BLOOD
ON THE
THRESHOLD

a novel

KARIN RICHMOND

LIVE OAK
BOOK COMPANY

Published by Live Oak Book Company
Austin, TX
www.greenleafbookgroup.com

Distributed by Live Oak Book Company

For ordering information or special discounts for bulk purchases, please contact Live Oak Book Company at PO Box 91869, Austin, TX 78709, 512.891.6100.

Design, composition, and cover design by Greenleaf Book Group LLC
Cover images: ©iStockphoto.com/Primeop76-C. Benavidez Photography; ©iStockphoto.com/cinoby-Tobias Helbig; Image Copyright sixninepixels , 2012. Used under license from Shutterstock.com

Scripture taken from THE MESSAGE Copyright © 1993, 1994, 1995, 1996, 2000, 2001, 2002. Used by permission of NewPress Publishing Group.

Cataloging-in-Publication data
Richmond, Karin.
  Blood on the threshold : a novel / Karin Richmond.—1st ed.
    p. ; cm.
  Issued also as an ebook.
  1. Victims of violent crimes—Psychology—Fiction. 2. Assault and battery—Fiction. 3. Dreams—Fiction. 4. Economic development—Texas--Fiction. 5. Texas—Officials and employees—Fiction. 6. Texas--Politics and government—Fiction. 6. Suspense fiction. 7. Christian fiction. I. Title.

PS3618.I34 B46 2012   2012951973
813/.6

ISBN: 978-1-936909-61-2
eBook ISBN: 978-1-936909-62-9

First Edition

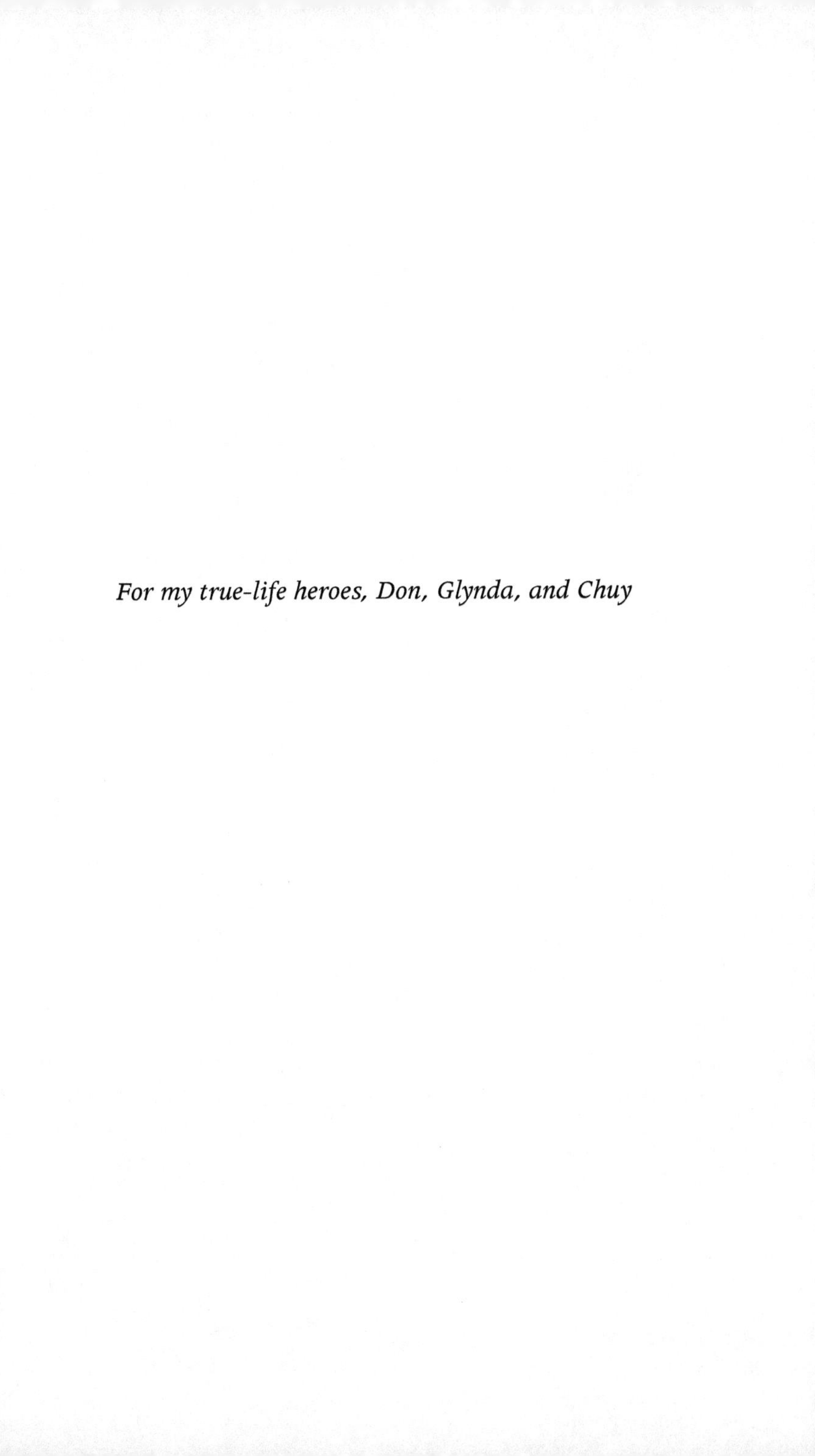

For my true-life heroes, Don, Glynda, and Chuy

AUTHOR'S NOTE

This work of fiction is drawn from real, actual experiences. The dreams were—and still are—real. Some elements are fictionalized, particularly in the minds of the assailant and those surrounding him. A few names have been changed and a few places renamed to protect the innocent—and the guilty

It is my sincere hope that other crime victims find courage from my story. We are not powerless. Even though our bodies have suffered assault, it is our strong spirits that survive and may even thrive. Our journeys are arduous, but we can emerge from victims to victors.

"We've been surrounded and battered by troubles, but we are not demoralized; we're not sure what to do, but we know that God knows what to do; we've been spiritually terrorized, but God hasn't left our side; we've been thrown down, but we haven't broken."

—2 Corinthians 4:14, *The Message REMIX*

PROLOGUE

The girl was resting on a spectacular lily pad in a serene body of water. The water was deep, way over her head. She felt relaxed, happy. The sky was light blue. Then an angular black man emerged from the depths and settled on a nearby lily pad. He fell back, struggling. He could not swim. The girl moved toward him to keep him from drowning. When she tried to guide the lily pad to reach him, hundreds of silver shiny knives came raining from the sky, now angry and dark. The man slid, slowly vanishing under the water, and she knew he was not to *be seen or heard from again. Turbulent waters whipped her around and out of control. Knives bore down on her, closer. Slashing, stabbing, and thrown by invisible hands. Blood turned the water deep crimson. She saw the knives relentlessly tear her skin.*

■ ■ ■ ■ ■

The same girl forced herself awake on her twin teen bed. Looking up at the bedroom ceiling her coffin appeared directly above her. She was convinced she was dead. Absolutely dead.

1

BORDER MELTDOWN

As it turned out, the telephone receiver lying atop the granite front desk of the historic Waller Hotel was a lifeline to the young woman who was about to be brutally assaulted. That young woman was me—Mirabelle Garrett. I was twenty-eight years old, exuberant, and in Austin, Texas, for a brief visit at the request of a Texas Senate committee.

I had worked for some time on an issue that involved certain tax benefits for companies that hired poor people in poor areas of Texas. The bill "had legs," as they say, and was positioned on the next morning's Finance

Committee agenda for testimony. I was prepared and excited. I knew I would be welcomed at the hearing. Still, I was nervously nitpicking my nose and scanning my written testimony.

Months of preparation had preceded the committee's invitation to provide testimony. The previous summer I had moved back to my border hometown from Houston. The impending oil economy collapse was on my radar due to a study I had recently submitted to an oil and gas client, but mostly I was worn out from the demands of the metropolis and needed some time to get away from a romantic relationship that had turned sour. Mom had welcomed me in her home, for the time being, and I set about networking in my newfound mid-sized community for a position where I could contribute toward positive social changes. I wanted a position that would provide me with the most credibility, the most visibility, in the least amount of time. My approach was simply that way. I did not want to lollygag when I was looking to be involved and engaged. I was ready and excited for action.

In a matter of weeks, I was able to convince the chamber of commerce president that the community was lacking a person in charge of economic development and that I had the skill set, I had the right motives, and I was a hometown girl who would work late and do whatever it took. But I would only do it for no more than three years. I had hopes of leaving the chamber and creating my own business based on the high profile I knew I would create in thirty-six months. Clayton, my new boss, completely understood where I was coming from—and where I wanted to go—and over the weekend agreed to bring me on staff as the Director of Economic Development, a brand-new position, the following week. But what a week it turned out to be for me and the entire community.

I started the job with the normal anxiety a new business role brings. I had already been in the offices over the weekend to get a feel for the place. I had a sharp new haircut and a new summer look. It was August in South Texas, the hottest time of the year. New people, new energies, new expectations. I was happy to be there looking toward a new horizon. I thought I brought a fresh, more urban, modern presence to this south Texas office. Chic business suits from Houston added to my look of exactly what a young woman leader should emulate: professional and capable.

The staff was competent and calm and generally a good group to work with. I especially liked Gloria, who was about my age and worked across the hall in tourism. Gloria had a bright and cheerful manner, but I quickly sensed a shadow underneath her smile. I found out decades later that Gloria was more than a bit jealous of my arrival and all the hoopla swirling around the "new girl." The old codger, Fred, who headed up industrial development—a rather dry field, in my book—was less than exciting. Tedious even. I had to respect him, though; he ran one of the nation's first foreign trade zones which was a very big economic achievement for our economy.

How could I possibly have known that within a few days on the job, an unexpected calamity was to strike at the heart of our city? Some radio chatter had been thrown around the airwaves on local talk shows, but not much warning was in the offing. Or at least no one saw it coming in quite the force and drama that escalated beyond control in Resaca, Texas.

I was in my office that morning when the news broke and the waves of press calls, starting from the East Coast, began to tie up all the phone lines. My boss was on the hot seat, and I could see he was talking to senior press correspondents from all the services. The previous night our neighbor city—ten miles away, but in a different country—had had an economic collapse that wreaked havoc with its purchasing power. Imagine a state university yanked out of a medium-sized city overnight. That was the severity of the situation. Many stores were to close and unemployment would reach a pinnacle that would take years to recover from. Urgency and underlying panic were prevalent, not only in my office but spreading all the way to Austin as well. My dress began to show my nervous sweat.

I went to the front receptionist and asked her to hold

our boss's calls. "I can't do that" was her hard-shouldered response to my request. But I was vexed, and persisted. "Hold his calls, please, after he gets off this one and until I get out of his office. I will take the blame if there is any. Now!" The receptionist reluctantly nodded her head this time, but I thought I caught a slight grimace on her face.

I waited outside his door until I heard the click of his phone hanging up and walked in. He looked a little dazed, but still calm amid the storm that had yet to show its true force. I flung myself on his prickly business sofa cushions and absentmindedly moved back and forth to scratch my back, ready to absorb this ad hoc lesson. "Let me help you, Clayton. Give me 'International Economic Development Policy 101' right now." I searched his expression. "We have about five minutes." He started to protest at the futility and thought perhaps how much he could trust me, his newest employee, in this very public position with only a few days' experience. Then the phone lines started lighting up like Christmas again. The blinking phone lines were unrelenting.

"Okay, here are the basics," he began with brisk intonation. "The value of the Mexican peso is in free fall. Mexican oil prices are falling, world interest rates are spiking, and the peso has been overvalued for some time now. The banks are scrambling and the Mexican government does not have the capacity to stave off this collapse." He went on with more depth along with adept metaphors and analogies to suggest as interview quotes with the press.

Within a few minutes, I was in my office assisting with the journal and television inquiries and getting into the fast-paced press deluge. The pace was almost overwhelming, and I loved it. How could I possibly have known that one result of this economic free fall would be my arrival seven months later at the Waller Hotel in Austin to do something I had never done before in my life? Essentially, the idea was to give tax breaks to businesses that locate and create jobs in places that have been hit hard with economic duress. How could I have known, while I was there doing public service, my fate was already in play in the halls of the hotel?

2

EARLY WARNING SIGNS

In Austin, the capital city about 300 miles away from the Texas-Mexico border, a human resources manager was frazzled. The clanging of construction equipment and hammers pounding on the floors above her were about to drive her to the loony bin. Her young daughter had been finicky about what to wear that morning and that had made them late for school—and work.

Deborah May was a seasoned professional and knew her way around an interview process. She had come on board with the hotel management team the year before, when the hotel was reopened after a several-million-dollar makeover. This historic hotel was on the main street of downtown and had a prestigious past. She was committed to ensuring that its legacy lived on through the employees she selected to make this place a home for visitors to the state capital. She was also very committed to securing a good position in the new company for herself. As a member of the ground floor management team, it was her job to lose and she had no intention of doing anything but the best performance she was able to do.

Deborah was a single mom, black, in her late thirties. She had about given up on dating men, but a fellow had asked her out to dinner the week before. Her aunt had suggested that the two of them get together, so she felt safe—both emotionally and physically—going out with him. He was in the asphalt business, with some ties to the little town of Crockett. She actually had a good time with the guy!

During the dinner conversation he asked if she "needed anybody" at the hotel. "Well, we are hiring right now, since the hotel is just getting opened up an' all. With all this construction goin' on downtown, though, I have a time finding some of the people I need."

"Would you mind takin' a look at a guy I know? He's not terribly skilled, but one of my team leaders is looking out for him since he just moved into town. His name is Leroy Johnson."

"Have him come by and I'll see if we have a fit for him," Deborah said with a smile, then took a sip of the full-bodied red wine. His grin was irrepressible.

■ ■ ■ ■ ■

A few months earlier, twenty-three-year-old Leroy Johnson had come to the capital city looking for employment. From a lower-middle-class background in Crockett, Texas, a small town about 100 miles away, he, like many others, had migrated to the closest urban area looking for work. He also had to get out of Crockett because he had a past to hide.

Later in the week following Deborah's romantic dinner, Leroy came by her office. His interview was short and perfunctory, and she had him complete an employment application. He seemed to be a quiet young man, very polite. On the thin side but easily six feet. She discreetly scanned his outward appearance. One can tell a lot about a person based on how he is dressed. His clothes were working man's clothes. Tan khakis, white button-down shirt, and a frayed brown belt. The clothes fit him loosely, like they were a size too big. "Maybe hand-me-downs?" thought Deborah. They were clean and pressed, though, she noted.

Her boss had called her into his office the day before and stressed the need for her to secure a full staff quickly.

Indeed, she was short in some of the "back jobs," those not directly in contact with hotel guests, and room-cleaning staff was a little thin. She could use some new hires to fill out her team.

After Leroy had left her office, the phone would not stop ringing. She glanced at his application and noted that he had listed two recent former employers. One was a fast-food chicken joint and the other was a contractor; neither was in this city. Both were in Crockett. "Was that the town her date had mentioned? Deborah asked herself. "Croc . . . something?" Didn't matter, though; he was still cute when she recalled his smile.

Background checks were essential in her line of work. Over the years she had realized that people can and do say just about anything on an employment application. Her own internal sense of ethics compelled her to be thorough with every applicant. She picked up the phone to verify the first employer Leroy mentioned and was listening to it ring and ring without answer when her manager waltzed in. Deborah put down the receiver and looked up with just a little impatience in her eyes.

"Give me some good news, Deborah. Our investors are coming in to see the property and how it will perform during our soft opening. What do you have?"

Deborah summed up the hiring situation and reported she was getting the staff in place. They went over a few other details for the opening, then left. Deborah glanced at her watch and realized she had to leave to pick up her daughter from school.

On her way out, she handed the application to the secretary. "Call Leroy Johnson. Tell him we can use him for room cleaning, maybe some room service if he does well. Oh yeah, let our security staff know about him—and the others we hired yesterday. Everyone needs uniforms!" The secretary nodded, but inwardly she was shaking her head. This office was a zoo with all that was going on and around so fast!

Calls to the two former employers Leroy listed were never made. Had hiring protocol been followed, Deborah would have found out quickly that these were false references.

In the following days, Leroy was a little surprised he got the job. After all, he'd served a stint in county jail and he'd made up stuff on the form. "But hey, man," he thought, "I ain't gonna ask no questions, no siree. From now on it's gonna be 'yes ma'am, no sir.' Keepin' the profile as low as it can go."

But some things just can't change in a man.

3

ENCOUNTER ON THE BACK ROW

New to the job, I wasn't new to the world of politics. I called our local state representative to have some margaritas and some strategy talk. They mixed well together, talk and tequila.

Frankly, for me, convincing Juan Hinojosa was the easy part. Juan Hinojosa liked to be called by his nickname, Chuy. He had been called that by family and friends for as long as he could recall. Many of us used it as a term of endearment. For Chuy was endearing. He was a calm, quiet man from modest Hispanic origins. He did not talk much about the war, but he was a decorated Vietnam soldier. When he came back home, politics beckoned him to help better the conditions for his people in his south Texas district. He could work with business interests and then party at pachangas with noisy mariachis and good, warm-hearted supporters—all in a day's work.

So, although I did not know him well in those early chaotic months following our August economic crash, I did know that he was passionate about his district and would work creatively and across party lines with Republicans to build back the local economy.

This public official was at ground zero in the aftermath of the economic collapse, after all, and anything of practical value was of importance to him and his constituents. I knew that and so did he. He agreed to introduce a bill early in the next legislative session, which began January 20th. The bill would provide for highly targeted tax breaks and he would work hard to pass it into law. But Representative Hinojosa worked in only one-third of the process. The senators in the upper house and the governor also had to get on board.

My approach to the state senator serving his south Texas constituency in Austin was a different matter altogether. He impressed me as someone very self-assured, and from my point of view, he certainly acted as if he were the most important elected official in the entire state. That wasn't the opinion widely held by others, however. No getting around it, he was a dashing presence and had an electric smile. And he had to be concerned with the economic recovery of his district and needed something in his legislative arsenal to at least have the appearance of acting on behalf of his constituency. I played to his ego, promising to make him look good and in charge of managing this difficult border public policy. He liked the "wonkish" sound of this.

So, for very different reasons in my mind, each of them agreed to support a legislative effort that targeted tax incentives for the border community. It was going to be a long and uphill battle in the upcoming Texas legislative session.

Over the years, I would reflect on my relationships with these two men. One moved from being a state representative to a state senator and sat on the committee that set the law for parolees and the number of beds in the Texas criminal justice system. Both interests directly affected my life in hugely important ways.

The other man retired from the Texas Senate and dabbled in politics and a little film acting. I still recall—with some bitterness—that for personal reasons he worked behind the scenes to prevent my ascension to a state board as a governor's appointee. But that happened much later, after I was to testify before the committee he chaired that April morning—without me. He was still spreading his power and charm around me and others and I was unaware of his unstated agenda. Consumed by the lobbying work, I did not see it coming.

My work to influence the governor and his staff was more circumspect, and as it happened, the key to this door was presented to me one afternoon in the back row of my community town hall during a presentation made by the governor—live on stage. I was pretty sure the governor was going to issue the same platitudes and the same false camaraderie I had heard a zillion times, it seemed. And, quite frankly, I had other things to do. But my boss cajoled me into going to the presentation. I grabbed my purse, slung on my strap heels, and walked over across the Spanish-styled plaza in the blinding heat and sunlight of the semitropical afternoon. I quickly glanced at my reflection in the solar glass as I passed an office window and saw my pink lipstick was perfect.

The town hall was modest, suited to our needs. It was newly built and had the latest technology in an amphitheater-style auditorium. Most of all, the air-conditioning was cool on my hot skin. Light was dim over the rear aisle. I took a quick look around and slid into the last row, leaving a score of empty rows between me and the nearest concerned citizens, each hoping the governor would give them a patrician glance. I touched up my face with powder. No telling who I might run into at these political gigs. "Be prepared for anything" was my Campfire Girls motto, and I held onto that mantra with hoops of steel. I took in the room. No one unexpected today. The usual city leadership men were up in front shaking hands with the governor—well, at least that is what I assumed.

I pulled out some of my light office reading material to try to make some good use of my time as the governor droned on the stage below. Not that I did not appreciate what he was trying to do; I had heard that particular speech sooooo many times and he was staying on message. I felt a light tap on my right shoulder. I looked up through the dim light.

I had no way of knowing, but there was someone else in the room who had spied me from a distance. As I was to learn later on, he was working in the background, running from his last meeting where quiet introductions were made among men in dark suits and white guayabera shirts, to get back into the auditorium to watch the crowd's reaction to the governor's message. Scanning the audience, he saw me—someone he considered a young, very attractive woman—my thumb on my chin, apparently deep in thought, but not on the man on the stage. He drew near and looked closer. Hard to tell why I was there. No name tag that he could see. But nice perfume. Being the curious man he was and a natural people person, he tapped me gently on the shoulder.

"May I sit here?" he asked politely, motioning to the empty seat right next to me. I slowly moved my eyes up into his deep green eyes and viscerally reacted to his intense gaze. My spine went taut.

I was a little puzzled, but flattered, as his intent was clear. "Sure, of course." I could tell he had been out in the tropical heat, too, as he still bore beads of perspiration on his forehead. "Not a bad package," I said to myself. He settled into the adjoining seat and offered his hand. "How are you?"

"To tell you the truth, I was a little bored . . . until this moment," I coyly replied. I tossed my hair, reacting to the tingle up my spine. I had not caught his name just yet, but didn't press. I would wait for the moment. "You are not from here."

"That's right, I'm from Austin."

"You must be with him," I said, my pen pointing toward the stage.

"Yes, and I am a little upset that you were bored with his speech!"

"Oh, brother!" I said, rolling my eyes and mimicking a deep southern accent. "Does he ever say anything different?" He asked why I was here and I said, "Under duress," with a little sarcasm in my hushed voice.

His eyes held a softer expression as he looked directly at me and asked, "What is your favorite thing to do in your favorite place in the world?" I was slightly taken aback, yet impressed with the question. "Now this is someone worth talking to!" I said to myself.

I was experienced for my twenty-something years and had enjoyed quite a few special places in my past, some that evoked exquisite memories. So I paused to think. I had to choose carefully with this man. "I think it would have to be walking along Seven Mile Beach in Cayman, playing my flute at sunset and wearing a silk flowing dress with no underwear on."

We both grinned at each other. I could tell he took an instant liking to me. "Go on."

Not to be taken in, I stuck with the game and asked, "How about you? Surely a handsome, educated man like you has had some delicious places to recall. What is your favorite thing to do?"

Being a sophisticated and professional man, wary of prying ears, he borrowed one of my manila envelopes and wrote on its back a provocative poetic reply to my question. Two sultry stanzas. I really had to stifle a little squeal of delight. I realized from his fleeting smile and a slight jut of his chin that he was impressed with himself for sharing a secret. Something he rarely did these days.

He looked up. His moment with me had reached an end, the governor was into the last section of his speech, the one my new companion knew too well. He felt like he had been on a mini-vacation, simply being beside me. Duty called. He pulled out his business card (I had never really caught his name) and scratched through the name and number of a law firm with some political acclaim.

"This is where I used to work, but here is my new number. Call me if I can ever be of any help when you are in Austin." Then he looked quickly to the stage and moved confidently toward his commander in chief.

I did not realize what had exactly happened; it was all too sudden and surprisingly intense. I turned over the card in my hand. The paper was stiff. The print was raised and embossed. I was unfamiliar with his name, but the law firm scratched out was internationally known. I placed the card in the inner pocket of my purse for safekeeping. I didn't realize until later that he had not returned my manila folder with the sultry poem written especially for me. But I could recall the stanzas word for word.

After a few handshakes with other attendees and a nod from my new friend, I almost glided back across the courtyard to my office, my spirits in a much better place. "How'd it go?" Clayton asked.

"Fine, nothing really new." I smiled to myself and hummed a few bars of "The Girl from Ipanema."

■ ■ ■ ■ ■

The next few months I was consumed with the development of an idea for Texas to grant incentives to companies to locate in poor areas. Nothing was straightforward as there was no legislation in the state code that resembled what I was trying to do. So I traveled to Washington, D.C., to a conference that focused on what other states had done in this tax arena in recent—very recent—years. A few other states—Virginia, Illinois, New York—had implemented their own version of inner-city revival tax incentives. And there was a whiff of federal interest in the rarefied D.C. air of a federal statute in the making. Eventually, it would become the Kemp-Garcia Enterprise Zone bill. And eventually it would become the law of the land, but I did not know that then. I did not know that I was to have a particular hand in the passing of that bill in the year to come.

Right then, I needed some examples of current state legislation to bring home for cobbling a legislative draft of a Texas bill. The bill I eventually pulled together was called the Texas Enterprise Zone Program. Before software was invented for a "cut and paste" editing tool, I literally cut and pasted the state bill together from copies of bills I collected in Washington. And can you imagine my astonishment when the receptionist called me up front for a "special delivery"? She was very curious! The draft bill for the Federal Enterprise Zone Program had been included in an upcoming congressional hearing before the Ways and Means Committee preliminarily scheduled for November 1983. I was floored and flabbergasted when I received my formal letter from the committee staff inviting my testimony. "Well, well, well.

Looks like I'll be spending some time in Washington next November!" I said aloud in response to the letter.

Over the ensuing months prior to the Texas Legislature convening in January, the day-to-day duties of my position kept me busy long hours. Intermittently, I would travel to both Austin and Washington, D.C., to attend factfinding meetings and gather political insight. I recall the Christmas that year was especially endearing with my grandmother hosting a large family soiree. The cool December weather was perfect for taking my quarter horse out for rides weaving in the citrus groves and under tall palm trees.

New Year 1983 came and went. The state legislature convened and I had already made a few trips to the capital preparing the politics and meeting with legislative staffers on the enterprise zone bill.

And now it was April, and what a fine spring day in Austin, Texas, it was. I was almost giddy when my chamber colleague walked me from the foyer to my room on the security level of the hotel overlooking the pink granite capitol building a few minutes before midnight—to be sure I was safe. The delegation needed me the next morning.

But violence intervened.

4

SECURITY MIS-MEASURES

Henry Gonzales had already made his security rounds throughout the hotel. He had gone over some bids for some upgraded security equipment he had suggested to the hotel management team. Sometimes running a hotel security department was paperwork, lots of paperwork. "On the other hand," he thought to himself, "the alternative to drudge paperwork meant something or somebody had broken his security protocols. And that would be a bad thing all around." He found some nearby wood to knock on for good luck. Being Catholic instilled a little superstitious behavior now and then. He chuckled at his own silly habits.

It was late in the afternoon, his legs were stiff, and his wife had called to ask him to come home early to help her at home. She was both his lifelong love and in chemotherapy. It hurt him to see her suffer as she endured the weekly rituals. She was taking the ordeal like a trooper and so, when she actually asked for help, he knew she was hurting beyond her normal pain.

Henry got up and decided to check out the kitchen and back areas of his hotel. Great smells were already seeping out of the kitchen as the sous-chefs were slicing and dicing with their flashing knives for happy hour hors d'oeuvres and dinner entrees. He grabbed a sausage and grinned at one of the chefs. "Better watch your waist, young man. You may have to run down a bad guy someday!" said the chef good-naturedly.

Going into the back pantry area, Henry noticed a recently hired room service employee. He searched his memory for his name . . . "Leroy. That was it," he thought. He nodded to Leroy, but Leroy barely acknowledged him and kept his eyes downward. Henry thought it was somewhat odd that he had a perhaps perloined large Tabasco bottle, but he assumed he was fetching it for the kitchen staff. The guy unnerved him for reasons Henry could not put his finger on. But it wasn't his job to do the hiring, and no one had asked him his opinion of the new housekeeper. After radioing his deputy with a "heads-up, you're on," Henry continued on his walk around the property and slipped outside to his car before the evening rush hour began in earnest.

5

DEADLY INTENT

As my chamber of commerce colleague accompanied me to my room, I was feeling especially good and somewhat heady about my role and the testimony I was to deliver in the morning. My friendly, outgoing smile was in full bloom and my sassy sense of humor in play. I was not shy in any sense as evidenced by my bantering with the hotel's bartender and the front desk manager earlier that afternoon, and now as I said good-bye and turned to enter my room for the night.

"Good luck tomorrow at the hearing!" he beamed proudly.

My comfy bed had been turned down—the fluffed pillows and chocolate all in order—but I noticed that the pink silk blouse I had asked the hotel staff to press that afternoon had still not found its way back to the closet of my temporary home away from home. "That's not a good thing," I thought. That was the blouse I had planned to look my very best in at the hearing in about ten hours from that moment. A little miffed, I picked up the bedside phone to admonish the front desk clerk, in a teasing sort of way, in hopes that my perfect pink blouse was en route to my room. I slipped off my shoes and noted once more the gold foil–wrapped chocolate on the fluffy pillow glinting in the bedroom lamplight. I deeply breathed in the dark hazelnut scent.

6

A CRIMINAL MIND

Life in Crockett had been simple. Small town. One high school. Friday night football was the social highlight of the week. Leroy was not much involved with the team, unless you wanted to call the occasional marijuana score for the players "involved." He was an angry young man, a small-time drug dealer who hung out on the sidelines of the field and, truth be told, on the sidelines of life. But he was fascinated by one of the cheerleaders and was drawn to her over and over again.

"Oh, lord, she is one tall glass of water. Uh-uhm. Can

just feel my hands runnin' through that strawberry blonde hair, her lookin' up at me with that radiant smile of hers. Sure does look good in those short skirts, showin' off those long, lean legs. Man, she make those gymnastic feats look so easy. Wish she'd try some out on *me*. And her breasts just perfect little teacups for me to lick the rim of. Every time she climb up on that team pyramid, her back all arched and legs spread wide apart, I can't take it. Gotta go under these bleachers and jerk off to get relief. That ain't right; I should be givin' it to *her*. Damn, why won't the cunt even look at me!"

Sometimes he would find a reason to bump into her in the high school hallways. Once he "accidentally" knocked her backpack to the hall floor. He picked it up in hopes of a friendly thank-you. But one of the football players called to her from across the corridor and she waved back. She gave Leroy no mind. Hardly knew he even existed. Leroy understood deep down that he and Catherine were miles apart, even standing next to each other between bells. His hurt from even a denial of a look from those green eyes stuck in his soul for a long while. His mama told him to forget about it and go on. And he did go on—for a time.

■ ■ ■ ■ ■

Several summers after graduation Leroy's life was still just slow and hot. A series of dead-end odd jobs and the occasional bag delivered in the shadows of the late afternoon. Got him by at least. One night, full of cicada buzz and sticky warm air, he eased up to the local EZ In store to grab a soda. "Shit, man, that's Catherine inside the phone booth." Cold sweat started running down his arms and neck. "Fuck! Thought I'd forgotten all about her but I sure do want that bitch now that I see her again. Want her to SEE ME. Want her to say hi and smile. Need her to taste me and cry for more of what only I can give her."

He leaned his rickety bicycle against the corner of the building and felt for the switchblade in his pocket. It felt so familiar in his palm. Leroy's ears picked up the click and he ran his finger against the sharp secure blade. Now he knew what he wanted to do. "I'll show you who I am, bitch. I'll show you I've got power over you, make you feel my raw strength. Teach you to look at me and show me some respect."

Catherine had her face to the phone and was completely unaware of the present danger. She had returned home for a short visit with her mom and brother. A nurse who now lived in Austin and had a job in an ER, she was talking to a girlfriend, a former cheerleader, and making plans to meet her later that evening. The conversation segued into a little trash talk about a mutual friend getting knocked up the previous month and speculating on the father. Leroy approached the dirty glass front door of the convenience store and moved as if to enter the building. The cashier had his back to the door, so Leroy seized the moment. Without any verbal warning, he reached into his pocket, pulled out the blade, and stabbed Catherine in the upper shoulder.

"Shit—what the fuck?" She dropped the receiver and it dangled from the pay phone, swinging side to side. Leroy raised the blade and stabbed her again, this time closer to her slender neck. She screamed and tried to push herself inside the booth for protective cover, but he stuck his size-13 boot in the door and pried it open. One more time, the blade hit her shoulder muscle, but this time when he pulled it back for another go, the blade broke and the knife hit the grimy sidewalk. Blood was oozing through Catherine's summer blouse. Leroy looked directly at her. "Leroy, what the hell?" She screamed his name as loud as she could. "She does know my name after all," he thought, and threw his head back and hooted. The cashier turned to the front of the store. Leroy took off and ran, forgetting the broken knife and his bike still leaning on the corner of the store.

Catherine's cheerleading chum was shocked by her friend's scream. It being the days before cell phones, she had to run to the neighbor's next door to call the police. The pay phone line was still open, the receiver—now smattered with Catherine's blood—dangling in the booth. "Thank God I told Kelly where I was calling from," Catherine thought as she slumped to the ground. The cashier was clueless, of course, because he had not actually seen anything and she had been lost from his line of sight. Leroy was long gone.

But not long gone from the police. The small town peace officers knew their citizens well, almost by name. And Leroy was a known small-time grass dealer. Didn't have a record—yet—but they kept an eye on him up through his last years of high school and beyond. When they got to the crime scene, Catherine was conscious but near a state of shock. An ambulance was radioed in. When she told the officers who had done it, each man knew where to start looking.

The police caught Leroy after a brief frantic scramble and placed him in the local jail. He was charged with assault with a deadly weapon, but his public defender succeeded in getting the charge dropped to a misdemeanor assault in a plea bargain negotiation. This was his first time to be actually inside a cell and, unbeknownst to him, the beginning of a long life of incarceration.

■ ■ ■ ■ ■

As Leroy would tell fellow inmates a few months hence, memories of that night in Crockett were running through his mind as he stood in the back pantry area of the hotel kitchen. He couldn't believe his luck in being handed this ideal setting in which to replay his vengeance against uppity white women—especially that bitch who ruined his life in Crockett. He had carefully checked the hotel guest list and found two promising possibilities. Both of the names on the registry were for a single-occupancy room, and both signatures appeared to be Anglo-Saxon surnames. "Maybe I'll get lucky," he said to himself, "and the one I pick will be as pretty and titty and leggy as my Lady Catherine."

His plan couldn't have been simpler. He would carry an industrial-sized Tabasco bottle in one hand and a black plastic garbage bag under his other arm. Both items were easily available to him as a room service employee, and they would neither be missed nor recalled as out of the ordinary should someone see him walking the hotel halls. He was wearing his white coat upon which his black plastic nametag was pinned. Leroy certainly looked the part of a hotel employee doing his job on an otherwise quiet Tuesday night.

Stepping off the elevator on the eighth floor, he glanced both right and left down the hallway. His nostrils flared as he prepared himself for the hunt. Turning right, he silently approached the first room and fantasized about the woman he'd find there—alone. His muscles tightened. His adrenaline started to pump. He felt for the familiar knife concealed in his pocket, the steady companion that gave him comfort and courage. He knocked firmly on the door.

A young blonde woman answered within a breath's

time. She had obviously just stepped out of the shower because her hair was wrapped in a white towel. Her guest robe was perfumed and soft to the touch. He knew just how soft and smooth because he pulled them hot from the hotel dryers every day. She looked quizzically at the room service employee. From the bathroom, her girl-friend called to her, "Who is it, Kate?"

Startled, Leroy quickly mumbled an apology, ducked his head, and got out of there fast. It was about eleven thirty.

A few quick steps back to the elevator and a short ride to the sixteenth floor. Checking the note he'd written on his palm, he confirmed the room number of his second option. The elevator door opened with a dull chime and again, checking both to the left and to the right, Leroy stepped into the hallway. His nostrils flared as he sharply sucked in the scents of the hallway. Stale food. Lingering perfume. Sweat. Air freshener he installed yesterday. The coast seemed clear. Turning to the right he began mut-tering to boost his confidence. "Okay, I'm feeling lucky. Feeling lucky, lucky, lucky. Yeah, man, the next bitch I find will be all alone in her room. All alone, man. Yeah, yeah, she's gonna be putty in my hands."

7

BLOOD ON THE BED

It was approaching midnight. The line was silent for a moment as Ted, the front desk clerk, recovered from my gentle admonishment about my pink blouse. He confessed that I'd caught him idly chatting with Chuck, the hotel's handsome bartender and—like Ted—an affable young man. It was a slow Tuesday night for both of them and they were looking forward to kicking back when they got off at midnight. Ted rebounded quickly and teased me, remarking, "Why do you have to wear that certain blouse anyway? You must have a dozen, at least!"

I stuck out my chin and hoped my mock defiance came through the phone when I replied, "But they're all home and I need this one, now!" I actually did have another blouse in my suitcase, but the soft pink silk one was the one that showed me off to best advantage, I thought.

Ted told me to hold on, he'd need to go check in a room behind the front desk for my blouse. He'd be right back. I overheard Chuck ask Ted what was up. When he found out who the person was on the other end of the line, the bartender teased, "Oh wow, if you find the blouse, let me take it up myself, Ted! Maybe I can get a tip or two!" Chuck hung tight at the desk, waiting to resume the pleasant midnight banter with Ted when he returned from his searching. The reception area remained quiet, and the receiver lay off the hook, on the counter, just inches away from where Chuck stood.

I held the handset loosely near my ear, and paced the floor. I wriggled the phone cord between my fingers and waited for Ted to return with good news about my blouse.

I heard a firm knock on my door. "Yes! There's my blouse," I thought. "What else could it be?" I tossed the phone handset on the bed, almost tripping over my shoes in my haste to get to my door. I opened it slightly to see who it was. (This was before peepholes were installed in that particular property.) I saw a uniformed black hotel employee who had a hotel name badge on his jacket. He held a garbage liner in one hand.

Now I am not racist as a rule, but something made me recoil inside. "Do you have my blouse?" I asked in a hesitant voice. I peered through the narrow opening hoping to catch a glimpse of my familiar pink blouse.

"No, no, I don't have any blouse, m'am, but did you order some Tabasco sauce?"

I looked at the large bottle of hot sauce, then glanced back to find this wary look in this strange man's eyes. My instincts were screaming at me to retreat into the safety of my hotel room. My eyes darted up and down the open slit of the hotel door. My breathing became short and my fear jolted me to slam the door shut. Too late.

This man, this stranger, pushed the door open, held it with his sturdy black leather shoe, and looked inside—checking for other guests, I presumed. Acting quickly, he swung the hot sauce bottle toward my face, connecting with my eyes and nose. The horrific impact sent my nose to the floor along with shards of broken glass from the bottle, now turned into a heinous weapon. The pepper chemicals burned both of my eyes, especially the left one, as he struck hard once again from left to right. It was a searing pain. He shoved me to the floor with brutal intent and kicked the door closed. I lost control. I was terrified and disoriented. I realized I was going to be raped and killed. The door was shut, my eyes were sightless, and an intense burning sensation was seeping into my skull.

I screamed as loud as my lungs allowed. As I learned

from Chuck later on, he stared at the receiver in disbelief as that scream from my room upstairs came through the telephone wire.

I pushed myself up with my forearms. "What are you doing this to me for? Why are you doing this?" I scrambled to my knees and, my hands already cut and bleeding, swept them gingerly over the carpet around me. I felt the jagged neck of the hot sauce bottle, grabbed it tight, and lunged upward toward my assailant. I could barely see shadows and light, but my thrust struck his forearm. My quick response with that errant piece of glass drew blood.

In the days that followed, I learned that, next door to my room, a newly arrived banker had been settling in for the night. It was almost midnight, and he was tired from the meeting and greeting required of an incoming president. Martin Daniel had slipped off his wingtip leather shoes and was easing his slacks onto the hanging butler when he heard a door slam hard and a blood-curdling scream. He thought he heard "RAPE!" but could not be sure. What he was certain was that something terribly wrong was going on within earshot.

Standing there in his boxer shorts, he did not take the second to pull on his pants, but he did put on his leather shoes and tie them tight before heading out his hotel door. Later he explained that he thought he "might have to kick a door down," so he needed his shoes.

Chuck, apparently, wasted no time either. After realizing that the scream was no prank, he yelled to Ted, "What room is that girl in? She may be in trouble!"

"Room 1605," Ted gasped.

The bartender spied one elevator resting on the lobby floor, its door open. He sprinted across the polished granite floor, jumped in, and slammed the backlit "16" button. Ted yelled after him, "I'll call security!" but the doors had already closed and Chuck heard nothing but the gentle whirr of the rising box. He had no idea what he was about to witness.

■ ■ ■ ■ ■

Behind the door of room 1605, I rallied against my killer, but I was forced back on the floor to my knees. Leroy must have anticipated finding a noisy victim because he had brought along a black garbage bag, which he stuffed deep in my mouth to muffle my screams. Apparently he was not interested in satisfying some sexual fantasy that night, despite his boasting, "At last a white woman on her knees begging me to stop!" What he must have been after, I surmised, was the rush of the kill that was fueled by both his rage and his sense of power. Pulling a knife from his black uniform trousers, he flicked it open and slammed me to the floor again. The carpet dug into my face wounds. He paused for a moment to relish his prey, then thrust the blade into my back. And again. And again. Repeatedly. I lost count. Then he heard voices outside the door. He had to because I heard them too.

I could not comprehend exactly what was happening to me. It was all happening so fast. It was all so bewildering. I was hurt, I was blinded, and I thought—felt—something dangling from my face. I thought it must be my nose—what else could it be?—and I had to gasp for air. I swooned when Leroy pushed the bag further into my mouth and down my throat. I was completely vulnerable, about to die. I had no control over what was to happen next. I shook my head and tried to push the black plastic forward, out of my mouth, with my tongue so I could breathe and not faint. Then I felt hard slug hits on my back, so many I couldn't count them all. "Why is he hitting me so hard? What is happening to me?" I said to myself over and over.

My body collapsed on the floor in a blood-soaked heap. My blood and my life were oozing out of me from the open stab wounds on my back. In a way, time had slowed down to a surreal pace. Blood was splattered across the bed, the carpet, the drapes, and the upholstered furniture. I began taking stock of my life.

And then an equally astonishing event occurred to offset the horror unfolding around me. One that would transform my life in a way I could have never foretold.

8

LIGHT OF THE FATHER

I was raised a Methodist in a south Texas small town. My grandmother was the church organist for some fifty years and my grandfather was a humble, God-fearing man who owned and farmed a ranch a mile out of town, a little north of the local cotton gin. My grandparents had met in that town. My grandmother, Elaine, was an orphan. Her father contracted typhoid and her mother died in childbirth along with Elaine's lifeless sister on the long journey to establish a new home in south Texas.

Elaine was raised in turn by her closest immediate

relatives, but her aunt supervised her day-to-day. My Great Aunt Harriet was a spinster, as unmarried women of a certain age were then known, but she had chosen to be a newspaper reporter for the local paper. Good-looking—some would say handsome—smart, and articulate, she found in Elaine the child she could rear and love in a south Texas society that would otherwise look down on an "unwed mother."

Elaine had a gift for music and began volunteering at the Methodist church at an early age. She met her future husband through music, as a matter of fact. As a young man, Clifford had come from Tennessee for the good hunting. "The doves were so thick you could walk through 'em," I remember my grandfather recollecting. But man cannot live by hunting alone, so Clifford and his father decided to open the first, and what came to be the only, theater in town. It was open air and showed first-run black-and-white silent films to enthusiastic local townspeople. He hired two women to open the theater: one to take tickets and the other to play the piano to accompany the film's moods and mayhems. Elaine played the piano and enjoyed it. She later grinned and said she thought Clifford might have liked the other girl more, but she left early and Elaine obviously had to play to the end. A budding respectful friendship produced one marriage and one child, my mom.

Mom did not raise me to be overly religious, but since

my grandmother accompanied the church choir, Mom joined and sang every Sunday. The older I got, the more hypocrisy I saw in the church members' behavior outside those sacred walls. As many teenagers do when hormone angst hits, I fell out of church activities. But I never stopped believing in God.

So, when I lay on that Austin hotel room floor, crumpled in a blood-soaked heap, face down, barely breathing, a wondrous light glided toward me. It was a diffused shaft of light that slowly approached me. (Later, in my many scuba-diving excursions and once while swimming near pods of humpback whales, I saw the same sort of diffused tunnel light under blue water, clouded by microorganisms, and managed a smile—despite the regulator in my mouth—as I recalled this fateful moment.) An inner voice resonated within my tortured body and extended this invitation to me. "Mirabelle, you may come up now and be with us!" The voice was so clear in my mind and the message so undeniable, I understood that this was a message from God, my Father in Heaven. I also knew down deep in my soul that I did not want to pass through that entreating light, mesmerizing and warmly beckoning though it was.

Even though I had not understood what had happened just moments beforehand, nor what the lasting physical effects might be—wouldIseeagain?wouldIbeparalyzed? wouldIlive?—I earnestly asked, "Do I have to go?"

"Not at this time, if you choose," replied the same clear deep voice.

"Then, I choose not to come, not at this time."

"We will wait for you." The powdery light shaft slowly receded up to a place beyond my room, beyond my blood, beyond my world.

I slammed back into my horrific reality and again heard the voices outside the door. My instinct flashed. "I hope these are the good guys, or I am dead." But, in that simple and straightforward manner, I had prepared myself with God.

Both Martin and Chuck told me later that Martin saw Chuck running toward him down the hall and waved him over. "What's going on?" asked Chuck, somewhat out of breath. Martin shrugged and said he had heard some screaming coming from behind my door. With one look and nod of agreement, both men start to shake the door handle, only to find it locked. They rattled the handle again and banged on the door. Taking turns, they yelled, "Open up! What's going on in there? Does anyone need help?"

My assailant and I both heard the men outside, and I could hear and sense him throwing his knife under the bed. Then he roughly pulled the black plastic bag out from my mouth. We both heard the voices demand again that the door be opened, louder each time. Then the door shuddered. Someone kicked it. Again. And again. Finally, the door came smashing down, kicked down by two unlikely rescuers who I later learned were the hotel bartender and the banker who was the guest in the adjoining room. Strangers in a very strange moment in time. But for me, heroes all the same!

The two men described the sight before them as being worse than a murder scene in a Stephen King novel. What wasn't blood was Tabasco sauce, but who could tell what was what? Walls, carpet, lampshades, bed sheets all spattered with red splotches. Remarkably, the good-night chocolate still sat on the plump pillow unscathed.

They stared at the black uniformed man who was gesturing wildly, leaning over me, a horribly wounded woman. "Lady, can I help you, lady?" The would-be heroes paused a moment to gain some perspective on what had gone on in the room. They looked at each other then turned back to the man hovering above me. "Move over there and sit down and stay down!" they both ordered my assailant in unequivocal voices.

Right then Officer Waters, an off-duty policeman employed by the hotel for security, arrived at the scene. He had rushed from the hotel garage and was accompanied by two other hotel security assistants. Upon arriving at the threshold to the room, one of the hotel's security men took one look and turned to throw up in the hall. Entering the room and quickly assessing the scene, Officer Waters sternly commanded the uniformed black employee, cornered and sitting down, "Don't move!" Then the officer instructed Chuck, "Call an ambulance!"

Waters took a deep breath and turned his attention to me, the wounded woman at his feet. "Help is on its way, young lady," he softly said in a slow Southern drawl. He kept talking in low tones, trying to prevent me from going into shock. He asked Chuck and Martin to get some water from the bathroom to wash out my eyes. He found a portion of my nose nearby on the carpeted floor and slipped it into an evidence bag. I was moaning, and kept complaining that my back hurt, it really hurt. So Officer Waters took a chance and rolled me partially over to get a look. He could see the cuts in my dress and realized with some dread that I had been stabbed repeatedly. It was hard to tell how many times. As Chuck shared with me many months later, Officer Waters sadly shook his head and caught the eyes of both him and Martin to show them. Martin heaved, nearly vomited. Chuck said he stepped over the fallen door and stood in the hall to get some air. According to Chuck's description, Leroy just stared calmly into space, his body limp. Perhaps he was anticipating the black vortex he was about to enter and would not escape.

Quiet moments passed, I remember, as we awaited the ambulance. There was nothing much to say. I continued to moan softly, still not aware of what had happened to me, only that I could neither see nor breathe. Officer Waters was whispering gently to keep me conscious . . . and alive. Finally the elevator bell chimed, and I learned with great relief that the ambulance staff were heading toward the open room.

"Okay, everyone, move out, we need to get her on the stretcher and need some room to work!" barked the lead man of the ambulance team. Waters told Leroy to stand up, then handcuffed and Mirandized him. That is when he noticed that Leroy too had blood on him, and looking closer found that he had some cuts on his lower left forearm. "Say, medic, this guy has a cut bleeding on his arm—I can take him in, though. The cut looks superficial." The RN glanced over and nodded in agreement and turned back toward me.

Officer Waters stayed behind to take another look at what was now his crime scene. Leroy remained calm. Waters scanned the room visually. There was blood spatter everywhere: the carpet, the draperies, the bedspread, the upholstered chair, the wallpaper. He bent down to examine a small bit of something. "Hmm, human flesh. Man, this scene is rough." As he and Leroy departed the scene for the hospital, Waters noted the blood spatter on the threshold of the door. He cringed inside. "Be sure to get this," he ordered the police photographer.

A few short minutes later, the siren was turned off as the emergency vehicle turned into the hospital. I was rushed to the emergency room. I thought I saw some bright lights, but nothing like the light I had seen in my hotel room, and I sensed that I had arrived in a place of safety. But I could neither see nor smell. It just *felt* like a hospital. Urgent voices calling medical orders confirmed medical help was moments away.

9

DÉJÀ VU

An attractive strawberry blonde–headed nurse took charge of my intake as a new emergency room patient. She told me much later that she had been an ER nurse long enough to have seen just about everything there was to see. She liked her job, although there were times—like that night—she was bewildered by what people could do to themselves or others, provoked or not. She noted the expensive ivory silk shirt and matching suit skirt I was wearing and thought to herself that this was odd, even in this place of work. Most bloody victims, at this extreme anyway, came from the east side of town. It was right after midnight and her buddy running the ambulance told her he had gotten a call from the upscale hotel they both knew well. Then she put two and two together and realized I was the victim he had retrieved from downtown! Catherine brought me to the rear of the emergency area, called the "crash room." There, hanging curtains surrounded each patient and it was somewhat quieter.

She began to cut off the silk ensemble, when I spoke! "Do you have to do that? I like this outfit."

Somewhat startled, Catherine replied, "Yes, I have to do it." But with calm assurance she promised to keep my jewelry in safekeeping. What she didn't say to me then, but did to herself that night, is that if she was honest with herself, she doubted I would live to wear them again. She nearly wept, but her professional demeanor kept her on task. She thought it remarkable that I was still alert. My face so terribly disfigured . . .

"Oh my God, has someone contacted a plastic surgeon?" she called out, frantically.

"Already on his way," came back the answer. She turned back to me and used the scissors to gently continue cutting my clothes from my body. Done with the front, she carefully turned me over on one side to cut from the back. She gasped at the wounds. And though she did not know me, Catherine really could feel my pain, as she herself had been assaulted just a year earlier. Again, heroically pushing her own fears aside, she focused on me.

She turned to the adjacent supply cabinet to grab a urine sample kit, but none was there. "Crap," she muttered, "I need to get that sample tested quickly." She flung the curtains aside, nearly bumping another patient bed in the open emergency ward.

That was when she saw the next emergency room patient, escorted by police, and felt her scissors leave her hands, clanging on the floor. Her blood drained from her face. "It couldn't be . . ." she thought. "It's just not possible . . . not here in Austin . . ." She literally could not breathe or speak. He was coming closer and closer to her. Just then he looked at her and she realized he recognized her immediately. He smirked and nodded her way with a haughty thrust of his chin. Catherine screamed and backed into my curtained-off area, recoiling.

I felt my bed slide sideways with the weight of the nurse's body suddenly leaning against it. The entire emergency staff turned toward her, not understanding what had happened. Catherine could do nothing but try to catch her breath and hold on to the bed rail to regain her composure. Still, no words would come out.

The surgeon in charge appeared just beyond my bed, looked at Catherine, still trembling, and then looked at the patient in handcuffs. Knowing her history, he turned and asked Catherine, "Was this the man who tried to kill you last year?" Catherine slowly nodded her head as Leroy continued to shuffle past her. No more sinister smile on his angular face, as he kept his face down, staring at the floor tiles. The surgeon took command of his emergency room and declared to the police escorting Leroy, "Do not let this man out of your custody!" his dark eyes blazing. One of the officers turned to him and said, "We have to; we haven't found a weapon of any kind. He's here until we can get him stitched up and out of our hands."

The surgeon looked directly at the lead officer and gravely told him about what had happened one short year earlier and pointed to Catherine. "You have got to be kidding me," said the officer.

"Absolutely not. You get some men to go back to that hotel room and *look for a weapon*! I guarantee that you will find what weapon he used to stab this woman," he nearly shouted, pointing to me. Both officers stared at me. This was the first they had seen of me and what Leroy, they thought, had done to me, but they had not yet seen it with their own eyes. The sight triggered a reaction from the police escorts, and they slammed Leroy up against the nearest wall, pinning both his arms.

Catherine advanced toward the prisoner. The escorts nodded to her in silent affirmation. "Why did you try to kill me? Why did you stab me? Give me an answer, please!?" she pleaded.

Leroy literally grunted at her face. "What that you do, what that you say? I do nuthin'!"

The lieutenant indicated to the sergeant to take Leroy on to the back of the emergency room and he stepped into the hall and clicked on his radio. Seems the police team had left the hotel moments before. No, they had not seen any weapon or anything that looked like one. "Go on back and look around, closely. This guy may have done this before and if that is the case we need evidence to keep him in custody." The lieutenant signed off and waited.

I coughed then groaned with sheer pain. The emergency staff attentions were redirected back to me. Catherine picked up the scissors and turned me over again to resume cutting my clothes away. I was conscious enough to ask if anyone had called my home. Catherine did not know, but asked whom they should call.

"Call my mother, in Resaca . . . 512-631-2242." Catherine wrote the number on the back of her left hand and motioned for the emergency room clerk to come over—quickly!

10

BLOCKED LINES

Scribbling the number down on a spare piece of paper, the ER clerk was glad to finally get a number to call the next of kin. The hotel did not have another number on hand, and the home phone number listed in the directory did not answer. She dialed the number. Busy. She dialed it again, still busy. That was strange, as it was nearing one in the morning. Still checking, still busy. She called over the surgeon and asked for advice. He knew Resaca was a smallish town, so suggested calling information to find out if there was anyone listed there with the same last name. Bingo. There *was* one other person listed. The surgeon placed the call himself, dreading what he had to say to the stranger on the other end of the phone.

"Hello?" came the bleary answer.

"Is this Mark Garrett?"

"Yes, what is this about?"

"Are you related to or do you know Mirabelle Garrett?"

"Yes, she's my sister," my brother replied, now growing a bit anxious from the caller's tone.

"I am afraid I have some very bad news. Your sister has suffered multiple stab wounds; we don't know how many yet. Her face has been terribly disfigured, and . . . we don't expect her to be alive when you get here."

Mark's adrenaline shot through him as he sat straight up and turned on the bedside lamp. "Will you repeat that, sir? Who are you and where are you and where is my sister?"

"I am Doctor Garza, head of the Breckenridge Hospital Emergency Room in Austin, Texas, and your sister is here. She has been brutally assaulted. We have very few details. I suggest you hurry."

Mark hung up and turned to Lynne, his wife of a year, and told her the news. "Does your Mom know yet?"

"I . . . I don't know, I forgot to ask." He hit the single-button fast dial dedicated to our mom; it was busy. "How in the hell could it be busy this time of night?" he wondered aloud.

Lynne was already putting on her clothes and getting out of bed. "We have to go over to your mother's. Maybe the phone is off the hook for some weird reason."

Clambering to his senses, Mark slipped on his jeans and polo shirt. Lynne bundled up their baby daughter and grabbed the diaper bag and some clean clothes. She realized they were going to be gone a while. The family jumped into the old Mustang Mark had restored. A '68 hardtop, it was in pretty good condition, and ran sweet. He made the muscle car run quickly that night to our mother's home. He pounded loudly on her door. Over and over.

She woke up startled almost half to death. The pounding kept getting more insistent. She flicked on the hall light and peered out the peephole to see her son, clearly distressed. "What has happened?" Mark told her. She felt faint. She leaned on the hall wall. "Why didn't you call me?" she asked.

"The line was busy," Mark replied, shimmying by her in the hallway to his brother's room.

"I was asleep, not on the phone . . . WARRRRRRRD!"— she yelled toward the rear of her home. Our youngest sibling, he opened the door to see what in the world was going on. He held the cordless phone in his hand. "Have you been on the phone all this time?"

"Well, sorta." Feeling a little guilty but not yet knowing why he felt that way. "I'm talking to my girlfriend."

"AT ONE IN THE MORNING??? Oh forget it. Your

sister has been hurt. Mark talked to the hospital. We have to go to Austin right now. Get some clothes and your shaving kit. Move it!"

All of the family trundled into our mother's Suburban, and Lynne dropped off the baby at her mom's. Mom's husband, Bob, took the wheel and tore out of town. They headed north, wanting, for once in their respective driving lives, to finally be pulled over by a cop for speeding so they could get a police escort for the six-hour trip. No such luck, but they did make it in just minutes over five hours.

11

OUTSIDE THE LAW

My father lived in California at the time, having retired from a base commander position in the Air Force. He was a successful military pilot during the Viet Nam era and had come out of it alive and educated in the ways of the world. He was not around much when I was growing up, and I realize, looking back, that that was by choice. Much better at siring children than he was at raising them, he was mostly a father who managed-by-exception. That is, until I got into some trouble, like veering on my motorcycle too fast on the military base streets or making too many B's on my report card. Otherwise, not much real attention was given to me.

He was born of a poor parentage, his father a plumber who was a recovering alcoholic, and his mother a God-fearing industrious woman who was a telephone operator in the era when calls really had to be connected and a caller could still ask her for "Mr. Conley, please," and she would plug in the line to his law office receptionist. Dad joined the military as a way out of his south Texas town via an ROTC stint in the Agricultural and Mechanical College of Texas, later Texas A&M. He was well liked and successful as a cadet and quite happy, all in all. He had moved his new pretty wife to campus housing. His daughter was born while he was a freshman cadet. That appointment got him off campus, along with a stipend. The early family years were the best, in retrospect.

Tough love was what he learned both at home and as a cadet. Be self-controlled. Take responsibility for your actions. Work hard and work smart. If you bend the rules, do not—repeat, do not—get caught. (Several college pranks, for example, were never solved by the administration.)

Sometimes, a person can never tell when a "life lesson" is going to leave an indelible print on their soul. Tough love was a lesson I learned one day riding a bus on the base with my father. I was but six or seven and waiting side by side with my dad for the bus that would take us to see a jet "fly-by" exhibition on the base. I was excited to go somewhere special, just with Dad, the sniveling kid brothers left behind. When the bus whooshed up, I was frightened by the sheer size of the machine and the noise and diesel smell, its tailpipes low to the ground. The door clanged open, and my father motioned for me to step up and climb on board. I hesitated; the stairs seemed awfully tall, and this was a new and disconcerting experience. I turned, "Dad, can you hold me and take my hand?"

"No, daughter, you have to do this yourself. Go on now."

I did not understand. I wanted my father to help me, to be there for me, to help me up the stairs. But he refused! I sat down on the curbside and started to cry. He did not comfort me, and the bus driver was getting impatient and revved the engine. My father pulled me up off the curb and toward the folding door. So I reached way up high for the interior railing and pulled myself up and onto the big black footstep covered with black rubber parallel ridges. I reached again and again, and after what seemed an eternity, I reached the top of the stairs and took a deep breath.

"Now go on, get a seat," my dad said, moving in behind me. When I reached an open space, I sat down on the blue vinyl seat, Dad sliding in toward me. But my little heart had been broken. I felt like my dad did not love me and that is why he would not help me. I didn't deserve help. He was not proud of me because I was a scaredy-cat.

I have never really forgiven my father for being so unloving that day. It would take three decades for me to even bring it up to him; it was so wrenching and heartfelt. Later, I understood that this was simply the first elementary step toward learning the eternal lesson of forgiveness my spirit had brought me on the planet for learning, through incremental experiences. I was too young to see it for what it was, tough love. My dad thought he was doing a good thing, making me go up by myself so I could do it next time, and the time after that, on my own. He wanted to build my self-confidence. He wanted to teach me responsibility. He wanted to teach me self-control. Even in desperate situations.

And indeed I did learn those lessons over the years. In fact, it was largely due to those lessons ingrained in my psyche that gave me the strength to not pass out on that brutal night. To keep my wits about me. To tell the first medic I could find that I was not able to draw in air, so oxygen was quickly brought to my lips in the hotel room. Honestly, it was the fresh flow of oxygen that offered me my first hope, my first glimpse that I might make it out alive.

My dad had yet to be called and notified by my family careening toward the capital city. It was in the early hours of the dark morning when he finally picked up the receiver and his son, who was calmer than his ex, told him the facts as Mark knew them. Which wasn't much.

When they hung up, my father placed one other call. That call was to someone who could take the guy out if and only if the system did not work to catch his daughter's assailant. The price was cheap, twenty-five hundred cash. He returned the phone to its cradle and walked out into the night to catch an eastbound plane. He had a quiet thought about his own mortality after settling in his seat. He hadn't ever contemplated his children's demise. Frankly, he had thought a lot about his own death over the orange gas–clouded skies of war. But not his own kids'. "*Que será, será*," he mused with his patent aloofness. God was not in his thoughts, nor prayer to anyone or anything. "Mere mortals are we," he thought, as the first of a few winks came to him on the plane.

12

NOSE BLEED

Five hours earlier, Catherine had recovered sufficiently to undress and redress me in a hospital gown and prepare me for surgery. "Have you found a plastic surgeon?" I heard her ask the clerk. As if on cue, Dr. Roberts smoothly strode into the ER, asking for instructions. It had been a very long while since Dr. Roberts had even been to this or any hospital. Alert, good-looking and very intent, he strode into the open area I was in.

I was later to learn that Dr. Roberts was a veteran of twenty years, with his own established practice in the capital city. Doctor to the very wealthy, he was either a current or past president of every significant medical board governing plastic surgery. So he was a bit out of his posh element in this public hospital. But what a smile and what a sincere energy he radiated toward all who were around him.

He bent over me to assess my wounds. Even he was taken aback at the violence perpetrated against me. He had the privilege to work in his private surgery rooms, with none of these uncontrolled bloody rips and tears of the flesh. He asked Catherine to move aside and nodded to the chief ER surgeon, whom he had seen occasionally at local Rotary lunches. He touched my shoulder gently. I did not recognize this new touch. I had no idea how fortunate I was to be under the care of this decorated doctor.

"Don't worry, everything will be all right. I am Doctor Roberts, your plastic surgeon. I will fix your face and your back so everything will be hardly noticeable."

"Are you going to work on my nose?" I whispered.

"Yes, of course, yes. But first I have to stitch it back on your face, young lady."

"Well, as long as you are going to work on my nose, could you take out the roman hump while you are at it?"

Catching his professional composure, and letting out a faint chuckle, he replied, "Now, don't you worry. We can take care of that roman hump a little later, and you will never know the difference!" (Over the years, the good doctor would tell my story over and over again. Here was this young woman, completely slashed and with little hope of surviving the attack, according to the head ER surgeon's prognosis. And yet, she was worried about the hump in her nose! "I'll be!" he ends the story, and still shakes his head to this day.)

As he gingerly set my nose back in place, he began to work his skill on my face. He had gotten so far as an initial setting, ready to begin more precise work, when the surgeon in charge reappeared. "Doctor Roberts, I hate to interrupt you, but we need to determine if this patient has any internal bleeding."

"Oh, I didn't realize that hadn't been done yet. I can't believe she doesn't have any internal injuries," he said as he turned his head and spoke quietly to Dr. Garza so I wouldn't hear just how dire my situation really was. Honestly, it was beyond remarkable that I was still alert and conscious. Dr. Roberts stepped aside to allow the surgeon some room to work. The surgeon positioned himself above my torso and touched my belly button gently. "Can you hear me, Mirabelle?" he asked.

"Yes."

"I want to see if you have any internal bleeding, so I want to make an incision, right about here," he said, touching my lower abdomen.

"I'm not bleeding inside. And I don't want another cut in my body because I know I'm in really bad shape."

Both doctors turned to look at each other, and then back to me with slight nods of disbelief.

"How do you know you don't have any internal bleeding, Mirabelle?"

"I would feel it inside if I did and I don't!" I asserted with all the emphasis I could muster. Needless to say, both surgeons were incredulous. In all their experience, neither could conjure up a scenario where a multiple stab wound victim—there were at least twelve wounds that they could count so far—would have no internal injuries. It wasn't possible.

I continued, "I have some pain breathing and it's hard to breathe, but other than that, I'm okay."

The ER surgeon stepped up. "Mirabelle, if you don't have any internal injuries that will be wonderful. But if you do and we don't find out right now, the repercussions may be very severe."

"How severe?" I persisted.

"Worse than the wounds you have now because blood inside your system can cause extreme problems later." He was growing somewhat impatient with my impertinence. He really needed to start now and look inside.

"How long a cut will you make?"

"Just a small incision, right under your belly button."

"You will never really see it after it heals," added Dr. Roberts helpfully. Feeling outnumbered and overwhelmed, I finally acquiesced, and Catherine administered the

Xylocaine as a local anesthetic. The ER surgeon made his incision with a fine surgical knife and inserted the plastic probe inside my tummy, maneuvering slowly between my internal organs. Dr. Roberts looked on. The ER surgeon kept probing deeper, up toward my kidneys and on to my lungs. The vacuum pump connected to the clear plastic probe hummed quietly. Both doctors watched the clear line intently for red blood to be sucked from inside but no blood came. They looked at each other quizzically with expressions that seemed to say, "Does she really not have any internal bleeding? With all those stab wounds? Could it be possible?" The ER surgeon maneuvered the probe more to the left, then to the right.

"Mirabelle, this is good news. You do not have any internal bleeding. You are a very lucky young woman!"

"Thanks, doctor. I knew that, though." I smiled as I recalled the Light and the Voice from the hotel room.

Dr. Roberts stepped back into the process and began the careful work of reattaching my nose to my face. When he had stabilized my nose, he then carefully turned me over, with the help of the ER staff, and wondered where to begin. I felt a liquid poured on my back and I howled. It burned like fire; was it raw alcohol? I pleaded for some painkiller. Something, anything.

Then the medical team began cutting an incision on my side so they could insert a probe into my lungs. I heard and felt the sawing of my ribs, the cutting into my lungs. I think I fainted momentarily. Enduring that procedure was the hardest part up to that point. You can imagine, lying there and having to hear your lungs being punched and sawed into, and being able to feel it the whole time. Soon thereafter, they gave me a sleeping drug and I drifted into unconsciousness.

■ ■ ■ ■ ■

According to conversations I had later with the ER nurse, much earlier Leroy had been escorted to the rear of the emergency room and was attended by another ER staff physician. By now, the rumor mill had informed this young doctor that this was the assailant of the woman who was the center of attention of the ER staff. The officer removed Leroy's cuffs and his hand and arm were examined. "Some stitches will be required," thought the doctor, but he was really taken aback at how much damage I, Leroy's victim, was able to deliver given the shape I was in! After a few minutes, he was through. The white bandage was a sharp contrast on Leroy's black skin. The officer waited patiently until the last bandage was secured, then took Leroy into formal custody. While he was waiting, he got the call from his lieutenant. "We found the bloody knife under the hotel bed. Book the bastard!" Unable to come up with the $50,000 bail, Leroy was held at the city jail on a charge of attempted murder.

My condition had stabilized after my surgical procedures and I was sent to the ICU, still under close watch. I stayed for three days. My blood pressure was good enough, I was conscious, but I still had trouble breathing. The reason for this difficulty was the several puncture wounds I had suffered in my lungs. Even though I survived this ordeal with no internal bleeding, my lungs looked like pin cushions as a result of the assailant's knife. The medical staff glumly announced, "She's not out of the woods yet."

13

NO BACKGROUND

Around the capital city the police radios had been more or less quiet as midnight approached. Members of the press corps monitoring the waves were quiet as well, some scratching away on the latest *New York Times* crossword puzzle. Occasionally there would be a drunken pedestrian arrest on the waves, but it was only interesting if it was a legislator too tipsy after a long dinner hosted by a well-funded lobbyist. Then there was a police call and an emergency medical services call and the press around the city perked up at the new development.

Mike Cox worked the night beat at the *American Statesman* and was the first reporter to arrive when the wounded woman was transported on a stretcher from the ambulance into the hospital. He only caught a glimpse of her bloody face. Mike waved over a homicide detective that he knew from high school and asked him what was going on.

"Bad deal, Mike. A guest at the hotel downtown was stabbed in her room by a hotel guy."

"What do you mean, hotel guy?"

"Well, he looked like a room service guy. He had on a white shirt and black pants and vest with his name badge—so yeah, we think he was a hotel employee."

"Did you see him?"

"Sure, we cuffed him at the scene and he's in a patrol car now coming over here."

"Why here?" Mike was jotting hurriedly on his long note pad.

"Not sure; he had some blood on him, but I gotta tell ya, there was blood everywhere—later, Mike!"

Mike checked his watch—it was nearly two o'clock. He went back to the hotel to find the reception area in a chaotic state. He spotted the night manager to get a statement.

"Did a hotel employee stab a guest of yours?" Mike asked the direct question.

"No comment." The hotel management was clearly

trying to protect its options and public image. The night manager seemed to reevaluate his response. "Johnson used to work here in housekeeping, but we fired him a week ago." Mike made a note of the change of comment.

Inside her office, Deborah May was devastated. She had been called out of her slumber by the junior security officer and was on-site surveying the brutal aftermath. The reports from upstairs horrified her. She unlocked her office door and nearly staggered to her knees when she flipped on the light. On her desk in plain sight was a paper that could bring her ruin.

Leroy Johnson had not been performing up to task over the previous week. He had seemed listless, distracted in his duties. There was one complaint from another employee who thought he may have smelled a faint marijuana odor coming from his body. When she had had a moment to check back into the file she had put together when she hired Leroy, she noticed that the form for former employment was not there. Her stomach had lurched and she dug further in the few papers that were there. "Oh, Mary and Joseph! No one followed up on a background check," she whispered to herself. This was not good, not good at all. She already had grounds to fire him, and firing him would get this incriminating file out of view. If she could get him out of the hotel, no one would have to know that the background check had been overlooked.

It took two seconds for her to get a blank dismissal form, fill it out in triplicate, and tear out the pink copy. She wrote a quick note to her assistant to place this paperwork in his punch card slot before she left for the night.

That pink slip was never delivered to its intended employee. That pink slip was the one still lying there on her desk. She stared, unbelievingly, at the document that was probably going to be her professional undoing. She cradled her face in her hands and wept, not only for her hotel guest who may or may not live but also for herself and, most of all, her daughter, who would suffer the consequences. Deborah would surely be fired, and if she had the courage, she would come clean with the management and tell them herself, face-to-face.

To her surprise a newspaper journalist forced the issue. A firm knock on her door only momentarily preceded the security guard slipping into her office.

"We got a nosy reporter in the reception area wanting to verify if it was one of our guys that did this. I know it was Johnson, 'cause I saw him in the room, but I thought that guy was out of here already." His eyes met hers and they both looked down on her desk. "Oh, no. Oh, dear God, no." His voice was shaking and he reached out to steady himself on an office chair.

"Well, was he fired or not?"

Deborah May knew she was on the line and what she said might very well impact her position in the hotel as well as her work in the human relations profession at large. So she stuck to the technical truth. "I signed Leroy Johnson's dismissal form this afternoon. Before I left and before he got here. It was supposed to be in his time clock slot before he clocked in at 6:00 p.m." Her eyes met his in a kind of helpless gaze. "But as you can see, it is still here, so he did not get the notice—which means he clocked in this evening." That is as far as she could go. She could not let herself say, "as our employee."

"Oh dear God, I don't think this woman is going to pull through," he repeated, more to himself than to anyone else.

14

HOMECOMING

About five o'clock that evening my family finally arrived at the hospital, and the morning edition of the local newspaper already featured some splashy headlines on both the front and the inside Metro section, complete with photographs of my heroes and my assailant. The hotel management was claiming they had fired Leroy that afternoon for undisclosed reasons. Obviously, he had come to work that evening at the hotel. But the facts would be sorted out in a court of law sometime later.

The community in south Texas was shocked. I was a

well-known public figure, active in economic development, so the news traveled fast. I had gone to the capital
city to lobby and testify and had joined several dignitar-
ies, including the publisher of my hometown paper. The
story was even carried in the Spanish newspaper that
served the neighboring Mexican metropolis. My boss
remarked in the paper the next day, "It's just sickening
when something like this happens. Not only is Mirabelle
a great asset to our town, she is also a good friend."

I was unaware of all the press attention I was about
to receive. The morphine drips had me in and out of
consciousness for several days. What I was conscious
of was this strange feeling an inch below my left lung
that had a fuzzy feeling, like when a person's hand falls
asleep. I rubbed along the area and there was no pain at
all, only a prickly feeling. I asked the doctors to look at
and even x-ray it, but there was no indication of injury
from a medical perspective. (A few months later, it was to
have profound implications for my spiritual connection,
which began from the Light that emanated from above on
the night of the attack.)

My family was all here, including my errant dad. The
woozy sensations started to fade and the pain of healing
set in like a vengeance. The expressions of sympathy, be
they cards, flowers, or visitors, began to flood in. Hundreds of notes and letters arrived at my hospital room.
My mother read most of them to me as I could only make

out the front of the cards with my damaged eyes. I was too scared to look in a mirror. I could not see at all from my left eye.

But oh, the flowers. Flowers were everywhere. I breathed the floral fragrances as deeply as my re-attached nose and punctured lungs would allow. And they kept coming. A huge arrangement was from the governor's office. My close circle of gay designer friends got together and sent a new spectacular arrangement every single day! My room overflowed with notes of concern and well wishes. Flowers were stationed on tables outside my door. "Every arrangement is for you, Mirabelle, and there are more outside. You must have a ton of friends and well-wishers. I have never seen anything like this!" my mother exclaimed.

I was simply overwhelmed. I finally began to open myself up to the crescendo of love energy that was being given to me but had not been able to recognize or feel because of the constant pain or the shadow curtain of the morphine. Tears came and came. As did a certain gratefulness for all this unexpected—and, in my mind, undeserved—warmth and support from family, friends, work associates, and even strangers. It felt like the warmth of God, like the Light from above. This time it was of this earth, not beyond. Here. Now. Still the tears came. Maybe . . . it was another way God directed to cleanse and heal my tortured eyes, looking back on it all. The fact I was alive remained a mystery to those who surrounded me.

My physical wounds healed superficially over the course of a few days—less than a week. The deep wounds inside my muscles were still painful. Still, I felt impatient to leave the care of the hospital and its helpful staff. When it became known that I was about ready to leave, my mother received a call from one of the wealthiest families in her hometown. Though my mom knew the name, she did not know the man with the slight Southern drawl speaking to her on the other end of the line. "I would like to offer the services of my King Air to get Mirabelle and her family home, with your permission, ma'am."

My mother was a little baffled, but she was always on the lookout for practical solutions to anything. "How terribly kind of you to think of us, Lanny. We would like that very much! I had not worked out how I was going to get her on the commercial airline yet, so this is really very thoughtful."

"Here is the number to call when you are ready," Lanny explained. "Let the pilot know when you want to go. Give him a little time to get the plane and the flight plans ready and leave the rest to me. I am so glad Mirabelle made it—she is a friend to me and this community!" Mom smiled deep down. She was proud of her daughter and relieved.

On a clear afternoon, I waved good-bye to the hospital

staff who had cared for me so well. "Keep the flowers." They were still being delivered to my room. "Please send the note cards so I can thank them when I am able." I tentatively turned from my bed and, with the help of two male orderlies, slipped into the wheelchair. Damn, it hurt to move. But I did, and made it to the private plane and finally to the private airstrip at home.

I was unprepared, though, for what I saw through the tinted windows of the van that drove me home. There were no less than three billboards that the community had erected welcoming me back! WELCOME HOME! WE ARE GLAD YOU ARE ONE TOUGH LADY! GET WELL SOON, MIRABELLE—WE NEED YOU! My family could not get over it, either, never having seen anything like it before.

Grandma reminded me that I was very special and very loved. "Now don't you forget that, Mirabelle. Times will be tough later on; hold onto this. In my life I have never seen such a demonstration of support, even when your Uncle Mike was mayor!"

15

FEAR DANCE

This dream has been a part of my psyche for as long as I can recall. I really think it is from part of another life or it is part of my soul life that reincarnates.

The glamorous scene was unexpected. I was on a dimly lit path and saw a long set of stairs toward a sprawling illuminated dance floor. The dancers were gliding to a waltz tempo in costumes that recalled Venice in a golden age. The music swirled and pulled me toward the dancers. Like Cinderella's transformation, my street clothes gave way to a full-length gown as I stepped up toward the piazza floor made of large alternating (chessboard) squares with Salvador Dalí curves rather than rigid right angles.

Along the back of the dance floor rose another set of decorated stairs topped with tall Corinthian columns made of white marble. They were symmetrically placed except for the center, where a larger open space begged you to enter.

And that is when he appeared. Standing tall and beautiful with long black hair. A prince among princes. He gazed at the dancers below and sighed. Our eyes met. He drew me to him as he glided down the wide staircase. Such an elegant man, but serious in manner and stride. Our bodies slowed as we drew nearer to one another. I took a long look at this soul entity and saw it was not a human man. But he was agreeable, nonetheless, and his energy fascinated my desire. He gestured to me with the movement of his arms, the breadth of his smile, and his wide, expressive eyes. "May I have this dance?"

I accepted his invitation and we joined hands and rhythms in three-quarter time.

For a few moments, I felt sheer bliss. Breathe deep was my instinct. "Deeper!" a voice was goading me on. "What do you see?" the voice pressed. "What do you feel?" it said, still persistent as we made our way around the floor.

His visage became more translucent and light patterns began to shift to my eyes. Now I realized he certainly was not human, but I stretched my neck and turned my eyes away from him to see in my peripheral vision. And that is when I saw that he was Fear. The realization threw a current through my body but I did not let go. He saw that I knew and did not draw away, nor did he hold my waist any firmer. It was I who had to decide how close I wanted to dance with Fear.

My eyes leveled with his as an unspoken mutual acknowledgment. I consciously understood that a kind of karmic lesson was presenting itself to me in this dream and I made the mental decision to continue in the dream state and not awaken. I wanted to dance with Fear for a few moments longer. I wanted to understand how I felt in the presence of Fear, and not bolt. I realized that Fear had created the music, the scene, my dress, and his vision to make me more at ease and allow me to come to him when we first met across the floor. This was a life lesson for me to embrace deep in my soul. When I was ready, the music stopped, the scene gradually faded to dark, and Fear as a flame placed himself in my arms. I moved away and awoke purposely.

"So," I mused, "it is possible to embrace Fear and even dance with Fear provided that I recognize the situation and don't fall prey to the 'flee' instinct." I pulled out my journal and captured the dream on paper. "This is a life lesson I need to remember."

16

NASTY HEALING

Over the course of the next several months, my mother, and later my close friends, took over my care. I looked like something out of a horror movie and moved with great difficulty. Demerol helped calm my deep muscular pain. My face was bandaged, and my back was covered by a huge sterile cloth supported by layers of sterile cloth bandages, all of which made me look and feel like The Mummy. I was so stiff. The scabs were beginning to form, which made it hurt worse. Pus was everywhere, it seemed. I felt like a leaky faucet. I picked at the scabs to fill the time.

Honestly, I didn't know what I felt like. I didn't like feeling at all. It hurt too much to feel. That unusual numbness persisted under my left lung, even more pronounced now. Poke. Poke. No pain but still there. I began to mentally process news items that got past my mother's firm and restrictive handle on her daughter's environment. Triage, in a way. Friends had been calling on me, but no, no visitors, not yet. I was glad to learn this because I thought no one had come by to see me. I realized later my mom was being protective. I was weak, more than I would like to admit, and still looked terrible.

But there were some pressures too persistent for even my mother's closed-door policy. The police and lawyers were lining up in the outside world asking questions, questions, and more questions. The good news was from the Texas legislature. My enterprise zone bill had passed both chambers! Wow! I was elated for the first time in what felt to be a very long time.

People recover and heal from vicious assaults in a myriad of ways. Some people even manage to grow from the experience. While I knew it only at a very deep instinctive level at the time, I began the long road to recovery both with the healing of my physical wounds and the emotional trench I found myself dug into. The emotional trauma I was going through was terrible. Prior to my attack I had a very strong self-concept and self-identity.

I didn't have any problem with me as a person in society and being accepted by it. I had to work through a lot during this time. The possibility of being considered an outcast, being considered—maybe—a wanton woman for letting this person in my hotel room. Being an outcast because of scars on my face and on my back. Being a freak in my community.

I returned to my work perhaps as a way to settle in and begin the healing process. That was when I began to hear the nasty rumors and whispered social chatter. I only recognized it in a vague way early on. But like a drumbeat the feeling bore down on me in the way people looked at me with sideways glances. The underbelly of the town— it was hard to pin down who, exactly—had a theory that I, in fact (in reality a fallacy), did know my assailant and I was "asking for it." I wasn't only stabbed but I "had" to have been raped and there was this cover-up going on. But "they" didn't believe it.

What finally became clear to me was an undertow of sentiment that followed the same "logic" as that of a woman asking to be raped because she was wearing a miniskirt. It was a kind of holdover from a male-dominated society where females themselves were to be blamed for both their contemporary self-expression and whatever resulted from it, be it clothes, choice of work, or outgoing personality. The last of the 1950s mentality that ostensibly guarded women and secured the male dominance in the world outside the home. It was a particularly nasty and ugly realization.

I wasn't as strong as I was used to being and I simply was not able to dust it off as I could before. It was so thoroughly untrue—not a shred of truth to it—and that was why it was particularly painful. "How could I be regarded that way?" I implored selfishly. Sassy? Sure! Outgoing? You bet! Flirtatious? Why not? I was smart, pretty, and single. But lurid? Absolutely not. Drag a complete stranger to a hotel room and ask to be mauled, stabbed, and nearly killed? What are they thinking?

I have to admit, I was taken completely by surprise with such gossip. My associates and friends blunted the torrid titters when they could and after a while they subsided. Later, when I befriended Catherine, the emergency room nurse, during the formal court proceedings, she shared that she had had to tolerate the same sentiments and same experiences from the "old white guys" in her small town. She was pretty, playful, and smart too. They meant to put her in "her place" as they wanted to put me in "my place."

"Maybe it's from a real desire to control or perhaps blaming the woman was the only way men from that generation could cope with such tragic victims," I speculated over and over to myself during the years when I tried to make sense of it all.

17

SUCCESS!

Life and healing progressed and work was a convalescent space, even at the frantic pace in the office. In a few months' time, I was back in the lobbying mode of my profession. I didn't have much choice and would have liked to jump back into professional gear more slowly, but the dictates of legislative and congressional calendars demanded a command performance before various state and national committees that had my tax incentive proposal on their agendas of formal deliberations.

Representative Hinojosa and the sponsoring state

senator decided on a two-house legislative strategy. That is, introduce the bill in both the House and the Senate and see which bill passed through committee hearings and full chamber vote first. Representative Hinojosa was able to get his version out first. Another state senator cosponsoring the bill motioned for the House version to be substituted for the Senate version, which was finally coming out of committee hearings. The House bill was voted to the full Senate floor where it encountered significant opposition from large city interests and regions of the state. We at the Chamber of Commerce had done our lobbying effort, and the Senators were informed. However, some serious concerns were expressed by at least two other senators. Interestingly enough, these concerns surfaced about ten minutes before the bill went to vote on the Senate floor. Staffers were running frantically back and forth from the lobby to the floor. We held firm on what we considered critical elements and compromised on sections we felt would not endanger the intent of the legislation. The compromises were accepted minutes prior to the bill coming to a vote.

Perhaps the most crucial blow to the bill was a floor amendment offered by Senator Farabee, making our act contingent on Federal Enterprise Zone enactment. A senator on the dais of the committee hearing room carefully explained that the state tax incentives of the bill did not become effective until the federal program was enacted.

Luckily, the final voice vote had the "ayes" carrying the bill. Now the bill was in Representative Hinojosa's chamber. He decided to risk a conference committee vote. The downside would be an enterprise zone act stalled in committee, effectively killing the bill; the upside was a strong independent bill to take to Washington, D.C., when we were to lobby the twenty-seven Texas congressmen for passage of the Federal Enterprise Zone Act. We successfully persuaded Senator Farabee to back off his amendment. The bill came out "clean" and was sent to the governor's desk for signature.

The biennial session was over, and the enterprise zone program had been passed by the legislature. Now all we—and the community I represented—needed was the governor to sign the bill. Word had come from Austin that he was not inclined to sign the legislation. He was a Democrat, and since President Reagan had already endorsed the Federal Enterprise Zone Program, he characterized it as a "damn Republican bill."

I called and then finally went back up to the capital and explained again and again the provisions of the bill to the governor's political advisors. Eventually, the governor changed his mind—oh thank you!—and signed the bill into law on June 19, 1983.

18

CONGRESS COMES CALLING

Far away from the events that surrounded my gruesome ordeal, the friends and leaders I had met in that 1982 Washington, D.C., conference had made some legislative headway with the Kemp-Garcia bill. One of the cute guys I had befriended was an unemployed journalist and sometime stringer who had now become a speechwriter in the White House. I had also been invited by a member of the president's cabinet to share my proposed Texas legislation with him and his intergovernmental team of advisors. That letter was buried in the stacks of mail thus far unattended. But, sure enough, it surfaced and I agreed to another D.C. trip.

Soon after arriving in Washington, I met the executive director of the Council for Urban Economic Development in his office. Mr. Finkle supported the bill and had agreed to accompany me to the Hill to explain my plan to various Washington elected officials. He had a quiet, efficient way around the marble corridors and knew many members of Congress who might coauthor this legislation. I, too, had already made many friends at the Capitol because they were from Texas and were aware of the pervasive and systematic economic stagnation that plagued their respective districts. So we were warmly received into many of the offices within the stately granite office buildings.

Only a few looked long and hard at my cane and wondered why I sat so stiffly, never leaning back on the chairs or sofas graciously offered to me. I couldn't. My back was too sore and still wrapped with layers of white gauze. What wasn't stiff from bandages was painful to the touch. I left all painkillers behind because my mind had to be on full alert. These senators and representatives did not have much time for anyone, much less for a woman who had never donated a cent to any campaign. But to their credit—or perhaps they were simply curious—each gave me a good half hour to present our Texas idea.

In the end, my work, with that of others from other

states and think-tank supporters, garnered sufficient votes on the necessary committees to bring it up for a formal hearing before the House Ways and Means Committee. I left the nation's capital deeply encouraged on a professional level. On a personal level, I was absolutely awed inside!

19

AN UNEXPECTED APPOINTMENT

Back in Texas, my work continued to be challenging. The legislative session and special called sessions had closed *sine die*. It was another hot, humid summer in south Texas. Resaca had struggled for a year or more to move from the economic mire created by the fall of the Mexican peso. I continued going to the office and working as hard as I was physically able. I had so much to do but was exhausted long before my work was finished in the time frame it required. I was always in a hurry, pressing the people around me to get off of dead center and follow my suggestions. Sometimes, at my desk, I closed my eyes and held my face in my palms and wondered if nearly being killed propelled me harder and faster than I had run before. I could not decide how much of it was me and how much of it was the looming legislative session or even how much of my strength was drawn from the appalling conditions that festered in the neighborhoods of deep and unabated poverty. I did not ponder long—the intercom jolted me out of my personal pity party.

"Mirabelle, line 2."

"Hi, this is Mirabelle."

"Hi, Mirabelle, this is John Fainter. How are you?" I recalled the state secretary saying.

I covered the receiver with my palm and held it away from my mouth to catch my breath for a moment. I casually replied, "Well, thank you, Secretary. A little hot down here at the border, sir, but that is no surprise this time of year."

"I understand you know a little bit about this bill on enterprise zones. Is that right?"

"Oh, yes sir, I know very much about that bill. In fact, I know the provisions inside and out."

"From what I have been told, I have no doubt, Mirabelle. Let me ask you something. Would you be willing to serve on the Board of Directors of the Enterprise Zone Program?"

I sucked in my breath. "*Indeed I would*, sir. It would be

my honor. And I think I could really help implement the program since I am also familiar with what other states are doing with their enterprise zone programs."

"Okay, then. Let me communicate your interest to the governor and we will see what happens. You are aware, of course, that this possible appointment is subject to senatorial privilege, am I right?" His tone was quite formal.

"Yes, I am aware that the senator from my district must support my appointment or he may use his senatorial privilege and vote my appointment down, and the rest of the Senate members will follow that lead as a courtesy." It never once occurred to me then and through the ensuing months that a senator would actually do such a thing. After all I had endured. I was so naïve in those early days.

"Thank you for calling me, Mr. Fainter!"

I jumped up from my desk and went running down the hall to my colleagues. Gloria was the first in the hallway to receive the news. "You won't guess who just called me!"

■ ■ ■ ■ ■

About two months later, I was driving my sporty Porsche 924 on the way to a city council public hearing. One of the items on the agenda was a motion to establish an enterprise zone in Resaca, Texas. The majority of the council was in favor. The mayor was adamantly opposed and believed that the council would obediantly follow his "nay" vote. I knew all that as I was driving down to the meeting. I had my radio on the local AM station and a newsbreak came on with an announcement.

"This just in, Valley. Our own Mirabelle Garrett, with the Chamber of Commerce, has been appointed chair of the newly established Texas Enterprise Zone Board. Congratulations, Mirabelle!"

I veered over to the shoulder and stopped the car, sinking into my leather seat. "Wow, this is amazing. I never believed this would happen. I've got to call Representative Hinojosa right away to thank him!" I paused my racing mind for a moment and realized the more important thank-you would be to the man who had handed me a scratched out business card so many months ago.

I blinked a couple of times to jolt myself out of my reverie and saw that the light had turned green. I floored the Porsche and zipped through traffic to City Hall. The business community had rallied. The council chambers were packed—standing room only. "Whew!" I blew out my breath and searched the crowd. Yes, both bank presidents were here. Good. Several business owners. My buddy and supporter Mike Blum from the City Utility Commission. The chamber president and my direct boss, Clayton, who immediately saw me and motioned as if to say, "Where have you been?" I flashed him an okay sign with the thumb and forefinger of my right hand.

I could tell that some in the room had already heard the news, including the city planner. She was pointing my way and whispering to the city attorney on the dais.

The meeting began in the usual way with the Pledge of Allegiance. After the minutes from the previous meeting had been approved, the only woman on the city council paused in the agenda to recognize my appointment. "Did I hear correctly that someone here was just appointed to the Texas Enterprise Zone Board?" she asked, smiling directly at me and giving a thumbs-up.

"Yes, ma'am but it still hasn't sunk in!"

"Congratulations are certainly in order," she continued, and every council member nodded in happy agreement. The mayor looked straight ahead over the crowd and was unmoved. Business as usual returned to the meeting.

At the posted hour for the public hearing, the mayor jumped over the enterprise zone issue to the next item on the agenda. I scribbled a note to the city planner that said this topic was formally on the agenda of a posted public hearing and the mayor had to call it. She took my note up to the city attorney, who read it, looked at me, and nodded. He went to the mayor and whispered in his ear while some other discussion was going on. The mayor's grimace spoke volumes.

"Well now," he began, "the lawyer tells me we have to call up this enterprise zone public hearing, but we can make it quick." His towering figure leaned far forward over the dais, and he swung his gavel like the rifle he was famous for shooting grackles with all over town. If "looks could kill" was the message in his glaring eyes that were aimed right at me. "I don't believe there is anyone here to speak on the matter. Am I right?" The crowd tensed. The mayor was a wealthy and powerful man and ran the city like he ran his multimillion-dollar agribusiness.

I sat ramrod straight in my chair and lifted my head up higher to face him. Out of the hundred or so folks in the room, I alone raised my hand to be recognized to speak. There was an audible hush in the room. "We know what you want to say, young lady," quipped the mayor. "We have already heard all about your tax favors and I am not inclined to give out tax breaks to you or anyone else for that matter."

"I still request to be heard, Mayor."

"Can't stop you, young lady, but you got three minutes tops." He dramatically scooted back in his mayor's chair, theatrically reclined, and lifted his wrist to eye level so his watch was clearly visible and the crowd could witness the charade.

"Then I will make it quick, Mayor," I began as I walked toward the podium. "I understand that your primary concern about the proposed enterprise zone is that it would give tax breaks, and you don't like giving out tax breaks in general. But that is not completely true, is it?" I looked him squarely in the eye. His wrist came down. "Last year the city gave tens of thousands of dollars to military veterans."

I paused because I knew my next sentence would provoke him. "In fact, you may be aware that the City of Resaca exempted several million dollars this year from agricultural interests, including yours. So you can't really say you are against tax breaks, right?"

The mayor blew up. He rose out of his chair and banged the gavel repeatedly, then hollered, "This hearing is closed." BANG! He turned to the council and asked for an immediate vote from the members. Slowly but surely each one registered his or her support for establishing an enterprise zone in our city. The city secretary called for a break, and I darted out of the building feeling like David who had just brandished his slingshot at Goliath. Wow, indeed! Resaca was going to create its enterprise zone after all.

Later, after the council meeting where the mayor's vote was indeed superceded, I was home sipping some wine and thinking back on the day. "One never knows what may happen. I sure did not expect today to turn out this way." I unzipped my office attire and slipped on my sleepwear. I winced when it caught on a swollen part of a deep scar still pink and tender. A small involuntary tear broke out on my face. I realized then that for a few hours that day I had forgotten my omnipresent pain. The adrenaline . . . I supposed. Now back to my bed and some well deserved sleep. "Oh!" I wished my cuts would stop itching and give me back some peace.

20

SPOTLIGHT IN THE CAPITOL

In mid-October that year, I was contacted by the U.S. Congressman representing south Texas. He called personally to let me know that the enterprise zone bill was scheduled for testimony in early November. He mentioned that I might expect a formal invitation to testify before the House Ways and Means Committee too. Wow! I mean Wow!

As I began to think through what I might say in the hearing, and how to best convey the urgent need for the proposed federal tax incentives, I thought that an elected official might be a more impressive messenger. On an impulse, I called my representative. "Is this the one, the only, the Honorable Chuy?" I was making a bit of fun.

"Oh, Ms. M. How are you doin'?" he asked.

"How would you like to join me in Washington, D.C., and testify before the Ways and Means Committee?"

He chuckled. "Going anywhere with you is always interesting. Sure, I will go with you!"

I thought he would be an excellent addition to the group as an elected official from south Texas, a Hispanic, and a person thoroughly knowledgeable about the provisions of the program. Now that he agreed, I had to work fast to get him on the panel to testify. After a few phone calls over the course of a week, I secured him a seat on the panel. I was having fun!

I touched base with my friend in the White House on my speech draft. Heck, he was a presidential speechwriter after all. We faxed drafts frantically back and forth until my friend and I were pleased with the presentation. I so looked forward to seeing him again! I felt a tingle of excitement at the prospect. He was one handsome and smart guy. "I could give him some extra squeeze," I thought wickedly.

When I arrived in Washington, I was interviewed by journalists interested in my story and my drive to convince lawmakers to implement the program I supported. I shared with them that many of us were convinced that an official designation by the state and federal governments to use this program would be the best approach to reduce the pervasive 20 percent unemployment of our area.

My piercing intensity underscored that the stabbing had more than a physical effect on me. I expressed to the writers that I realized that anything can happen to anybody, no matter how outrageous it might appear. And if a person has a goal to achieve, there is no time to waste because "you can get run over by a truck tomorrow." I was uncomfortable about talking about the incident, but wanted to go on record so that others might understand what I had been through and might realize that a brutal assault did not necessarily mean a person had to retreat from life, a full life. "Now, there is a cautious edge to my personality that was not there before, but I am not going to let it beat me down. Before this happened, victims of violent crimes were just a statistic to me; now they are very real."

■ ■ ■ ■ ■

The big day arrived. I had slept only in fits. I was thankful I got any sleep at all. This was my first time out of town since my assault and I would not—could not—consider a hotel room. I called my Aunt Jane, who was a U.S. Army colonel stationed in the area. A smart and spry three-pack-a-day smoker, she had a caustic wit honed from years of being the only woman in groups of army officers.

Jane picked me up at the National Airport and helped me with my bags and into the car. We were both excited and running over each other's sentences. When we arrived at her home, I eased myself out of the car and stretched as well as I could to chase away the cramps from sitting so long. Her roommate greeted us at the door. In the foyer, I glanced in a large Japanese framed mirror and noticed my facial powder around my nose needed a boost. My nose scar was a little more red and aggravated than usual. Maybe it was the stress of the altitude, or the stress of my first air trip. Anyway, I felt safe now.

Over dinner and a glass of wine, we got caught up and then Jane threw out the big question. "Did that guy try to rape you?"

Unfortunately, that was a question that was pressed on me in virtually every conversation or formal discussion about the assault. Over time I became less offended by it.

"No, it wasn't a rape. He didn't seem to have a sexual motivation, or maybe he did not have the opportunity. All I knew was that plastic was being stuffed down my throat and he was hitting me on my back. I did not know he had a knife until much later in the hospital."

With kindness and concern, my aunt shepherded the conversation to the next day's events and ushered me up to the spare guest room early in the evening. I was asleep before my head touched my feather pillow.

Jane crept back in later to take the outfit I had hung on the mirror door into her room to iron. I had selected a smart black and white herringbone fitted jacket, white blouse with a fluffy oversized bow, and a slim black skirt. My shoes were black, flat, and very sensible. Jane approved.

The next morning held crisp fall air, and the last remaining autumn leaves were clinging to bare trees. Remnants of Halloween decorations were on the occasional porch and a few trees still had tissue paper waving about between branches. My aunt dropped me off at the door of the U.S. House of Representatives. I found my way around the stairs to an elevator. The chatty attendant saw my cane and realized I needed a little extra time to ease into that tiny space. Although I dearly wanted to proudly ascend those white stairs to the building, I needed my strength for the testimony. I made my way through the corridors and met up with State Representative Hinojosa in the Texas congressman's office. The ubiquitous stacks of proposed bills filled the cramped outer office. Congressman "Kika" de la Garza came out to greet us both with a wide warm smile. His chief of staff, Cecelia, came to the reception area as well, with big hugs all around.

Our small entourage visited quietly in his comfortable

inner office to touch bases, then we gathered our files and followed the congressman to the Ways and Means Committee room. My first impression was how cavernous and spacious the room was. I looked up and appraised the very high ceiling before my eyes swept the crowd. There appeared to be several panels of witnesses called from all over the country. I scanned the room for other women and found two or three shuffling papers. As the panel before mine concluded, the representative and I whispered encouraging words to each other and approached the table.

The committee clerk called aloud for Ms. Garrett and State Representative Juan Hinojosa. I was listed on the agenda first and I adjusted the slim flexible microphone to suit me. I impulsively chose not to read my written statement, preferring to engage the committee instead. Congressman Rangel was vice chair at the time and was leading the witness panel. His sanctimonious attitude was almost palpable when he called my name. I looked to my left and to my right at the panelists already sitting in their places. I was the only woman to testify on that bill that day.

Ms. Garrett: Mr. Chairman, a year has passed since the fall of the Mexican peso. Rio Grande border communities have yet to recover from the devastating effects of the 1982 devaluation. In Resaca, Texas, unemployment remains rampant; last month our area experienced 25 percent unemployment, the second highest in the nation. Retail trade, our second largest employment sector, continues to suffer a 35 percent decline when compared to October 1982. In actual dollars, this represents a loss of almost $200 million from our local economy this year alone.

This situation is not likely to improve without help. By the year 2000, we estimate Resaca and the Rio Grande Valley will need 160,000 new jobs only to maintain our crippling unemployment rate.

How can we create these jobs? There are two basic alternatives: Public infusion of grants, loans, or payroll or, alternatively, private investment into our local area.

If local government officials were offered the choice between long-term permanent jobs and high levels of federal assistance, they would choose the jobs. There is certainly no magical remedy affixed to our tax dollars between the time they are taken from our pockets and the time they are redistributed to our ailing and distressed areas. However, there are some rather obvious implications in giving tax credits to those who hire the disadvantaged and who invest in distressed areas. First and foremost, unless a business actually creates jobs and makes new investments in the enterprise zone, there will be no tax credits given.

Mr. Rangel: Representative Hinojosa, do you want to supplement the Resaca testimony?

Mr. Hinojosa: Thank you, Mr. Chairman.

Mr. Rangel: Do you represent Resaca?

Mr. Hinojosa: Mr. Chairman, I represent District 41 in the Rio Grande Valley of South Texas. I will be brief. I was the sponsor of the State Enterprise Zone of the State of Texas and it was passed this past session and it received bipartisan support. There was not a single dissenting vote, and we had a Democratic governor, Mark White, who signed it into law, and it went into effect approximately 60 days ago.

Mr. Rangel: You are the only one on the panel that is an elected official. You have a constituency similar to mine. And your governor sets up a board to review the applications?

Mr. Hinojosa: That is correct.

Mr. Rangel: Has he appointed members to the board yet?

Mr. Hinojosa: He is in the process of appointing the members.

Mr. Rangel: Is it likely that you would know anybody on that board?

Mr. Hinojosa: Yes, I would.

Mr. Rangel: Ms. Garrett, are you going to help the representative in getting one of those enterprise zones in his city?

Ms. Garrett: Yes, as much as I can.

Mr. Rangel: You are a very lucky representative. I wish I shared the support you have.

He grinned at his own remark.

The testimony went very well, and Congressman Rangel had clearly warmed to our plea. My impulsive choice to talk to the committee instead of reading my testimony as the others had done before me had been wise. The conversations were engaging and resulted in an important change in the bill: a requirement that in order to actually get a tax benefit, the business must hire, train, and retain at least one-third of its new employees from among people with low-income backgrounds. It's all there in the Congressional Record. My work impressed someone in the room. As I moved from my panel table to the back of the committee room, someone from the Office of the President asked to speak with me. He asked if I was going to be in town the next day and would I be interested in joining the president to speak to this issue. He further explained that my south Texas companion and I were among a very few folks who were invited to the Roosevelt Room at the White House to brief President Reagan on their ideas for tax incentives to reinvigorate poor areas of the nation. I mused that my friend, the speechwriter, may have had more than a little to do with the invitation. The quick kiss I gave him surely had nothing to do with it . . .

■ ■ ■ ■ ■

Later that evening, Chuy Hinojosa, Jeff Finkle, and I had a small celebratory dinner in a famous but subdued dark paneled drinking establishment. We debriefed the day, joked to ease our tensions, and ruminated on the sidebar conversations we had had out of earshot from each other. Jeff had some particularly good suggestions for Chuy and for my next steps in D.C. We would have to do most of them from our home base in Resaca, where both of us had pressing business engagements, Chuy more than I.

On the way back home, I grabbed a copy of the *Washington Post*. One of the lead stories was about a new king coming to power in the remote country of Nepal. I thought about Mount Everest and imagined the craggy mountaintop. Was it like the Shangri-La of legends? "Why did that story catch my interest?" I mused, having never been to that bucolic yet rugged part of the world. Later on in the quiet moments during the flight—and later still in contemplative soul-searchings—my gratitude for all of those who had helped me and for all the serendipity that seemed to fall my way stretched out beyond my being toward the angels I just *knew* were hovering close by.

21

DEEPER WOUNDS

I could not or would not sleep in hotels for many months. When I finally did, it was only after meeting the security personnel directly and putting the management staff on notice that I felt unsafe in general and required a room across from the elevator. That elevator in the Waller Hotel being so close to my room is part of what saved my life, so I was sticking by that strategy.

My mental anguish could be consuming if I let it. Sometimes, I felt this overpowering blackness wash over me like sinking mud. But still I struggled with my emotional pain. I had vivid dreams most nights. I even revisited in my sleep a horrifying dream that took me back into the household when I lived with my family on a military base in Oklahoma. I was a young girl of thirteen.

> *I was resting on a spectacular lily pad in a calm body of water. The water was deep, way over my head. I was relaxed, happy. The sky was light blue. Then an angular black man appeared on another lily pad. He fell, and struggled. He could not swim. I moved toward him to keep him from drowning. When I tried to guide the lily pad to reach him, hundreds of silver shiny knives came raining from the sky, which had turned angry and dark. The man slid, slowly vanishing under the water, and I knew he was not to be seen or heard from again. Turbulent waters whipped me around and out of control. The knives bore down on me, closer. Slashing, stabbing and thrown by invisible hands. Blood turned the water dark crimson. I saw the knives relentlessly tear through my skin.*

I forced myself awake on my twin bed. Looking up at the bedroom ceiling my coffin appeared directly above me. I was convinced I was dead. Absolutely dead. When I got up and went into the hall, it felt like another parallel world. Colors were sharper, even in the dark. Sounds were crisper. I turned on the house lights. I felt the walls and the plastic light switch covers. Perhaps I was not dead after all? I went to my parents' bed and poked them to see if they were alive.

"Mirabelle, what's wrong, honey?" my mom mumbled, still not fully awake.

"No, nothing, I only wanted to see if you were still here."

I returned to my bed, rubbing my shoulder along the wall of the hallway for assurance and wondered what had actually happened.

Now, these twenty years later, I recalled that dream and understood for the first time that it was a precursor of the events that came to pass. But I could not have known that then.

■ ■ ■ ■ ■ ■

I didn't fight the inevitability of traditional psychological therapy too hard and made the usual appointments with a counselor over the course of most of a year. But the truth was that I never really felt as if I needed it. I was dealing with the emotional trauma in my own way. Maybe it wasn't the "best" way, whatever that was, and maybe it wasn't conventional either. But I did what I did.

I had made two deep internal decisions. The first and most fundamental conclusion was that I was not going to live the remainder of my life as a "victim." This wasn't as easy a choice as it might sound on the face of it. In the days after my assault, it sometimes seemed like my circle of friends, family, and community would be willing to accept caring for me as a "victim," if that was what I chose to do. At times I suspected that they predicted this, even though no one actually said anything. My outward lame appearance was disturbing to some. I was still walking with a cane, covered in scars, constantly in pain, and effectively blind in my left eye. I had no way of knowing just how much these injuries would heal over time and how many scars I'd be left with. But even given all that, I made my choice: the scars, be whatever they may be, I was going to go on with my life. Even more, someday—I didn't know when—I might even try to give some kind of support to other people who'd been through what I'd been through. I knew that was far in the future, but I knew the feeling was definitely there.

The second choice I made was to separate, as sharply as I could, my emotional trauma from the immediate demands of the situation—in other words, how I'd deal with the legal consequences of what had happened. Justice and legal authorities were in contact with me on a regular basis; my day in court was fast approaching and lots of people wanted details, details, details. Now. Now. Now. I gave them what details I could: I would sue the hotel in a civil court, and I would participate in the criminal trial that I hoped would put my assailant behind bars for a very, very long time. I couldn't ignore the demands these legal battles imposed on me, but instinctively, I found I could shut off the emotional demands of my trauma from my daily routines. It felt like slamming two thick, impenetrable doors over my psyche. Boom! Shut. Done. Onward.

■ ■ ■ ■ ■

A few years later, I found myself gliding up on a very steep and fast escalator in downtown Moscow. The subterranean subway tunnels doubled as underground evacuation facilities the Soviets had built during the Cold War, a vast complex comprised of tunnels dug deep into the ground under the city. These tunnels were meant to protect from nuclear fallout for those citizens who could make it down. Ingeniously, the Soviet urban designers had constructed a citywide subway within the tunnel system just in case the warmongers failed. (It was completely free of graffiti, I remember thinking wryly.) But as I rose out of the escalator and left the dark deep corridors, I saw the passageway I'd have to go through in order to reach the busy commercial street. Recessed on either side of the opening were two sliding *heavyblackthickmetal* doors. It took me a minute to recognize them. It was a kind of epiphany: Finally I knew, seeing those doors, what I had done—what I had slammed shut inside of myself during the early months of my healing. And yet, these doors were wide open, as if to suggest *my* heavy black thick metal doors might be opened—but not yet.

■ ■ ■ ■ ■

Though I didn't yet have that specific image of the doors, I expressed that feeling of absolute segregation to my therapist very early on. My doctor tried to pry the doors open, or at least to get me to talk about what those doors meant to me. She was using all the right technical jargon, but I would have nothing of it.

"I really have closed the doors on this assault," I told her as I sat on the upholstered high-backed chair in her office. "I know I cannot confront it now, or probably for a long time. But I feel I will be able to someday; not now, though. Not now."

My voice trailed off, then I continued. "I don't know if it's the right or wrong thing to do. And I don't know if it will stunt my emotional growth, or even perhaps my ability to love in a full fearless way. All I do know is that this is what I must do, for now. Later, I'll strive to pull the doors apart from each other and let the hurt back in. But that won't be for a very long time."

The session was over. I thanked the doctor, and I assured her that I would call if I needed her, that I knew she was there for me anytime. But that was the last time I talked about the event to a professional, until I was called to testify in court.

Still seeking truths or absolutions or reasons why this man tried to kill me, I explored palm readers and the *curanderos*, or psychics, who practiced their ancient ways along the Mexican border. That search brought me to Esperanza, one such curandera who was well known among the medicinal plant healers, the elder physical therapists familiar with meridian energies, and even a few of the health food proprietors along the southern border. Esperanza had a warm countenance and worn brown skin. Her eyes were like deep earthen wells. She quietly welcomed me into her small home.

"Can I offer you a cool drink?" she asked. "A Coke, some tea?"

I welcomed the tea and sat in a living room replete with Virgin of Guadalupe shrines in all shapes and sizes. Crystals and dried plants were strewn from the kitchen to the dining table. Herbs growing in the back were visible through the sliding glass door. The air smelled faintly of cumin.

We began to chat. Esperanza did not know why I had come to her, but she could sense from my energy that I had gone through something terrible and painful. She also sensed that I was not a quitter, but she suspended judgment as to whether or not that was a good thing.

She gently cupped my hands into her own and peered closely at the lines in my palms. A low whistle escaped her lips.

"*Andele!* We have something here, *mi hija.*"

I leaned forward with renewed interest and concern.

"You see here," she said, lightly tracing the lines

etched in my palm, "this is your life line. It is very long, but it is broken—see—*aqui*—look!"

I had never considered my hands, much less my palms, in this light. I was here to get a spiritual reading, not a palm reading. So what was all this?

"You know," Esperanza continued, "these lines are placed here in your hand at the beginning of your life by God. They are only yours, like fingerprints. But they can tell you many things about your life—what has been and what is to come."

She showed me her own right hand. A long deep line began between her right forefinger and her right thumb, and continued, etched into her palm, all the way down to the top of her wrist.

"You see this line?" she said. "I am to become an old woman with a full life. I cannot tell you that this 'fullness' will always be a good thing"—she smiled—"only that when I was born, God told me that I was going to be on this earth for a good long while." She paused. "Now look at yours."

My lifeline did not look a thing like hers. Until this moment, I had never really noticed that my lifeline was broken. Split in the middle. Busted. A clear breach, not to be mistaken.

"*Mi hija*, you either have or will have nearly been killed," she said, just like that. "There is no question. Is this why you came here today?"

I nearly fainted. "You mean that these marks are like a way to tell the future of a person's life?" I asked.

"It is not that simple, Mirabelle," Esperanza said. "You see, these marks tell about what our character can be or will be. They can also tell us something about our lives. Will we be happy or sad, divorced, blessed with children? There are many ways palm lines can communicate to us. There are also many interpretations about these things. One thing is for sure, *mi hija*—there is no mistaking this cut in your lifeline. Since you came into this world, it was foretold you would nearly die. But see right here—your lifeline continues. It was foretold that you would nearly die—and that you would come back to us!"

There was no mistaking it—just like there had been no mistaking the Light I had seen in that hotel room.

■ ■ ■ ■ ■

I met another profound woman, Lynda, who would influence and guide me for the rest of my life.

It was on a warm afternoon in an outdoor café immediately outside the long shadow of the single tall building in downtown Resaca. Lynda was holding her own sort of court in the patio as she often did. She and a locally admired artist, renowned for the use of brilliant hues of red, orange, and purple, were scheming how to raise money for local charity through art. Deep in conversation,

Lynda was throwing out some ideas when she could not help but see her lunch companion blanche in the warm air. Both of them watched as my mother and I carefully made it over to a nearby table and I eased down into the chair. I still hobbled with my cane and had a black eye patch over my injured eye.

"Who is that?" Lynda asked. "What happened to her?" Before she could finish her sentence, her artist friend had left their table and was talking to my mom, whom she apparently knew quite well.

She returned to Lynda, shaking her head. "That poor girl. She was in Austin and was hurt terribly in a hotel. I know her mom, so I wanted to say hello." Her friend relayed the story as best she knew, but still shook her head silently.

Lynda was deeply moved, especially looking at my face and sense-feeling my physical and spiritual strain. It was not until much later that she and I would forge a remarkable friendship that ascended into the spiritual realm that neither of us could imagine on that sunny patio. Lynda was the person, years later, to connect my childhood lily pad dream with the hotel assault and then quietly urge me to consider what it might be like to forgive my assailant. That would be a long time coming, though, with many surprising twists along the way.

22

SEX AND SOUL HEALING

Talk about information overload. I returned home from my reading and collapsed on my mom's navy leather couch. My wounds still hurt, so Esperanza's pronouncement was like rubbing salt on my skin. I was tired, tired, tired. And now I felt like I was at the precipice of insanity in asking why, why, why? Why me? Why am I even alive? Why was my spinal cord not severed; why were the deep cuts and slices between every major organ in my torso and not one was actually penetrated? There was no internal bleeding—what are the odds of that? Why did I have that dream about dying from knives raining from the sky when I was a child? And now this. My lifeline foretold of this episode—or something like it, I thought—and I had the message inscribed on my hand my whole life?

I slept on the couch. I could not even move at that moment. Then came another dream, another message, it seemed, from God. Another revelation.

I was alone walking from a wooded area toward a deep chasm. The trees were darkish foliage and the chasm was lit with the orange hues of late-afternoon daylight. The split in the earth was wide, as wide as the Grand Canyon. But the black depths had no end. Something in my soul knew it reached below this earthly plain into the confines of Hell itself. The fall would be infinite and final. The darkness beckoned me, closer and closer, to the edge of the vast canyon. The pull was undeniable. Come, come. I hesitated.

In a flash, I burst into red, yellow, and orange flames, yet remained firmly anchored on the rim. I had no limbs now, only an amorphous feel to my body. The call to the blackness below was more strident, menacing now. Part of me wanted to go; it would be so easy then, to give in, not to fight anymore. The tiny bits of flame from what used to be my hair succumbed to the pull below. More and more flames joined the first strands until my flame body was nearly off the cliff, falling forward.

Suddenly, a force within me snapped and the orange flames turned to a hot white light and ricocheted me back from the edge of the rim and back into my physical body. I stood up straight and tall. Held wide my arms, my white flaxen robes fluttering in the wind, reminiscent of angel wings I somehow had known before in another time and place.

I woke upon my couch bed and for the first time felt calm and serene.

I felt, finally, that my soul was on the mend.

■ ■ ■ ■ ■

Work was helping and I was well enough to return to my own townhouse just down the palm-tree-lined pathway from my mom's home. I started going through the motions of housekeeping and doing my little bit of gardening in back. I loved my brilliant red ginger flowers and the stunningly gorgeous orange petals of the poinciana tree I had planted after returning from a Caribbean diving trip.

But all was not well. There was a part of me that had yet to be healed, a part deep inside of me that had not been assaulted in a physical way, below the scars and wounded muscles. When I dared to bring it up to myself, I thought, "I am a monster. I am wrapped up in bandages seeping yellow matter. I am ugly, I am repulsive. I hurt so deeply. But this cannot be who I will turn out to be. This is not what I want to become. I want to be a full person again. I don't know if I will be strong enough to do this transformation by myself."

What I needed was a friend and a lover I could trust to bring me back to my state of grace. Joseph was the one. The only one. My pulse quickened when I remembered the first moment I laid eyes on this exotic man. No other way to describe him other than a vision in a 1930s vintage tuxedo. He was tall, all smiles, with shoulder-length wavy light hair, blue eyes, broad face; an Amsterdamman, dashing like the Gatsby was sublime. His energy radiated up and down the aisle of the church in a matrimonial procession.

He was escorting the mother of the groom down the aisle in a white stucco Mexican-tiled church. She was wearing a red taffeta full-length gown, looking beyond splendid. She was radiant. Joseph conveyed that he was ecstatic to have the most beautiful woman in the world on his arm. Years apart in age, their eyes nevertheless reflected a joie de vivre which threw energy sparkles around the pews much like the rose petals that were scattered before the bride and groom.

At the receiving line, after the ceremony, I approached Joseph and asked him to marry me—right then and there. I had not met him formally, did not even know his name. I was starstruck for sure!

Over the ensuing years, Joseph and I had many great excursions and much excitement together in our lives. Romping across the Mexican border was fun and always a bit risqué. Joseph was an exuberant host at his theme parties. At his Blue Martini party, for example, manikins were on display as "art" in the front lawn and crowds of real people were in the back.

Here I was now, needing him to give back some of that joy—that passion for life. I walked outside to my garden among the soft rattles of the palm trees. Mink, my brown Burmese cat, was outside in the tall ginger flower garden and greeted me with his soft call. I surprised myself when I decided right then and there to call Joseph and ask him to come over. He arrived, late as usual, and brought a single tightly rolled joint for us to share. He somehow sensed that a little relaxation was in order.

"How are you feeling, my dear—meds got you going through all this nonsense? Don't get so melodramatic, it will pass and you will be your old self in no time."

I gave into the smoke and his impossible eyes. "Make love to me, Joseph. I really want to do this now."

"Let's just take it slow and we will be all right." He gently moved toward me and in a dramatic flourish lifted me up and carried me across the threshold to my designer bedroom, complete with backlights, etched glass, and remotely controlled window coverings.

"I'm not going to ask a second time, Joseph!"

He grinned. Carefully and slowly he made love to me. I was playful in return where my body permitted. All in all, both of us saw stars that night and I was feeling much better about myself.

"Was that okay for you? Not too weird?"

Joseph replied, "Don't worry about a thing. You know me. I am trisexual—I will *try* anything once, twice if I like it!"

23

LEGAL MATTERS—THE COURT AND THE VERDICT

"All rise." The husky Latina bailiff had to raise her voice to be heard above the din of conversation in the courtroom. It was September and the Texas heat had not yet let up for good. The room was crowded, wooden benches almost full on either side.

Martha shifted her thick thighs to ease standing for the judge as he entered. Her arthritis encroached her ankles. She didn't have time for those "mid-life crises" she read about in movie tabloids at her east side grocery. She was too damn busy just trying to get supper on the table for her kids. All six of them. And now this.

Martha was in this capital city courtroom and not happy about it in the least. Not only did it take her from the housecleaning job she had held for twenty years; she had also had to get up before dawn and get her sister to drive with her in time for the ten o'clock opening of the court for this case—the *State of Texas v. Leroy Johnson*, her twenty-five-year-old son.

She knew why her son was in court. He had begged her to come, and swore he was not the one who had committed this crime. Well, his mama was no fool; it still struck deep in her heart that this was his doing. This was not the first time. "Dear Lord," she prayed silently, "this ain't the first time this child done hurt another person. I remember when Officer Holden showed up at the screen door last year lookin' for Leroy. Oh, lord Jesus, I know he's not the sharpest knife in the drawer. The boy coulda used some help—the mental kinda help."

Officer Holden knew Martha well and knew the trouble she had seen with Leroy. He knew she was truthful and a good woman. The rest of her five kids were good kids. A testament to her strong Christian values.

There was no bail bond money, so Leroy was forced to stay in the city jail until the Crockett judge could hear his case. *People of Crockett v. Leroy Johnson*. The hearing was pretty cut and dried. Catherine, the emergency nurse, was the key prosecutorial witness, with the store cashier chiming in what he saw and heard. Security cameras were hardly in the big cities, much less in Crockett, Texas. Leroy was charged with assault and battery and convicted of a felony aggravated assault with a deadly weapon. He started doing time in the county jail. No money to pay a fine or restitution this time, either. Martha visited him and brought him some of her red beans and rice—the guards weren't too fastidious with the visitation rules. And she always brought a Tupperware container full to share with them. She hated to see him that way, and still knew that something in her boy's brain just wasn't right. Nothing to be done now anyways.

Her daydreams back to that county jail cell were interrupted by a rustle of movement in the front of the courtroom and a newcomer to the wooden bench across the aisle from where she was sitting. It was a white woman about her own age. They each gazed hard in the other's eyes, somehow knowing they were connected to this proceeding but without knowing why. Yet.

■ ■ ■ ■ ■

This was the first time my mother had ever been in a courtroom. Sure, she had gotten one or two traffic tickets, but that was the extent of her experience with legal proceedings. She had arrived within minutes after the judge had walked in, having had great difficulty finding a parking place near the courthouse. She was wearing a dusty rose coordinated separates outfit, definitely fashionable, definitely comfortable. Jeanette—Dr. Cole as she was formally known—ascribed to the dictum "form follows function." Her stylish home reflected that philosophy, as did her outlook on life. She was practical in nature and that influenced all of her life choices.

But some situations were foisted on her. Like the one she was going through at this very moment. She had known her daughter to be a very independent thinker and doer. She had been a difficult girl to raise during her teenage years, both in California and in Oklahoma. Jeanette and her former husband had not parted well, and she noted that he was not present in court that day. "I would be surprised if he was here," she sarcastically noted to herself.

The past six months had been exceedingly hard for Jeanette to endure. She had kept her daughter close to her in her home and cared for her. When Mirabelle Garrett came home to heal, the lacerations on her body and her face distorted with swelling and stitches were almost more than a mother could endure. Mirabelle could do nothing for herself other than barely walk a few feet from one room to another. She was listless and barely able to eat on her own. Jeanette bathed her and cleaned the oozing from her scabs every day. Slowly, her physical wounds healed and she thanked God again for allowing her daughter to live and survive this attack. That son of a bitch needed to be put away by this jury. He could be put to death as far as she was concerned.

Jeanette looked at the judge and the lawyers who were quietly conversing at the front of the courtroom. The lead attorney for the prosecution had an air of authority about her, and Jeanette took some comfort in that. After all, it was she who was going to convince a jury to convict this . . . this *animal* who had maliciously attacked her daughter and nearly killed her.

A door opened and the courtroom stirred. A hand-cuffed man in an orange prisoner uniform was led to the table where the defense attorney stood. Jeanette did a double-take. "My God in heaven, he hardly looks human . . . more like a . . . a . . . some subhuman species." She had already grown to hate this man, but now that she saw him in person, she recoiled deep, deep down in her soul.

"Your Honor, may we approach the bench?" The district attorney confidently strode toward the seated judge. Straggling behind her, looking fairly out of sorts, was a younger man, counsel for the defense. There were some inaudible murmurs for a few minutes, and then the judge declared loudly to proceed with the case. Dr. Cole felt much better about the situation now that she had sized up the opposing counsel.

Leroy's mother shook her head. She might be unedu-cated, but she was a good judge of character, and this— "What they call it last time . . . pro bono?" —young attorney man was going to be no match for this hussy attorney woman. Martha sighed and settled back on the hard bench. "Lord, my boy needs help and this man does not look like much help to me." She stole a glance at the white woman across the aisle. There was something about her, but she could not put her finger on it.

Across the hall from the courtroom, I sat in an anteroom. A guard stood outside the door to ensure that I was sequestered. I was flipping through the most recent issue of *The Economist*, my absolute favorite magazine. It wasn't so much the heavy economics indicators I liked as it was the sly British sense of humor sprinkled in the stories and the perspectives about American politics from across the pond.

I was fidgeting, anxious. My muscles still hurt inside my body. My skin wounds had closed and the stitches had recently been removed. But I felt itchy and uncomfortable every time I twisted, turned, or moved even a little bit. I felt alone and vulnerable in that air-conditioned room. Too cold, but the chill made my scabs a little more bearable. I was nervous and checked my face powder often to do what I could to cover up the really nasty scar over my nose where it had been sewn back on. Damn, it still hurt. So tender.

And I had to face the court, the judge, and all those people who were strangers. But most of all I was deeply frightened about finally facing him, the assailant, eye to eye. Nailing his ass in court. But even with all the protection the court officers could deliver, I was deeply terrified of seeing him again. My primal fight or flight instincts were on high alert. I took a deep breath, and absently flipped through more pages.

■ ■ ■ ■ ■

The district attorney began to call her witnesses. She was methodical in the persons she called to the stand: the police at the scene, the ambulance attendees, the emergency room nurse, the hotel human resources manager, the hotel general manager, the hotel security, the hotel bartender, the front desk manager, and the banker who interceded. The questions were matter-of-fact, impersonal even.

When she called the banker to testify, he was nervous. Martin Daniel did not make eye contact with Leroy or his family at all. He hardly glanced at the jury. "Can you please state your name and address for the court?" asked the attorney. Martin hesitated. He knew what this man was capable of and feared that his family might be capable of desperate retribution. Martin had a wife and family to protect—what if they came after him? "Would you please state your name and address?" insisted the attorney.

Martin took a little gulp and answered the questions. One by one, the examination drew out the story of how he heard a scream from the hotel room next door, and threw on his shoes, then ran out his door. Together with the bartender, he kicked in the adjacent door and saw Leroy, moving away from a mutilated woman. A large broken Tabasco bottle with jagged edges lay on the carpet. Leroy made no attempt to escape, just slumped against the wall and slid to the floor. The men stood over the woman and ensured that Leroy remained on the scene until the security staff and police arrived.

After the questioning, Martin quickly left the courtroom. He was still deeply affected by the trauma, the horror of what he had seen and felt when he entered that neighboring room. That shocking memory would never leave him in the years to come.

As the prosecutor proceeded through the list of questions she had prepared to ask Catherine, the ER nurse, her mind was racing ahead. "There isn't another opportunity for the court to hear how she knew Leroy before," she said to herself while she flipped the pages of her legal pad. "Maybe I could simply ask if she knew Leroy prior to seeing him today in the courtroom." But the prosecutor knew the defense would object and the judge would agree—and might even slap her with a warning. Catherine had made no eye contact whatsoever with Leroy in the courtroom. She was visibly anxious. And as the prosecutor was winding up her cross-examination, she noted that Catherine was more jittery than when she had first taken the stand. "Nope," she decided. "I've got this case on other solid evidence." She concluded questioning the witness with nary a mention of the horrible stabbing in Crockett.

After the witnesses had each been called and perfunctorily cross-examined, the district attorney asked the judge for a brief recess. There was one final witness to call to the stand.

The prosecutor's stride was confident as she left the courtroom and nodded to the guard posted by the anteroom.

■ ■ ▉ ■ ■

I was pacing the floor now, my magazine rolled up on the table. She had to prep me for the stand. I was anxious and tense. I needed to settle down and focus. So the D.A. went through her questions, and I practiced my responses. Thankfully, the questions were few and direct. No emotion involved. At least on the surface.

"All rise," repeated the bailiff. The lawyers were in their places and the judge sat down and looked across the crowded room. He nodded to the attorneys to proceed.

"The prosecution calls Mirabelle Garrett."

"Can you state your name and address for the court?"

"My name is Mirabelle Garrett and I live at 800 Pinnacle Drive, Resaca, Texas."

"Where do you work?"

"The Resaca Chamber of Commerce. I am the Director of Economic Development."

"Were you staying at the Waller Hotel on the evening of April 6, 1983?"

"Yes, I was."

"Can you briefly describe to the court why you were a guest of the Waller Hotel that evening?"

"I was staying at the hotel because I had been invited to provide testimony to the Senate Finance Committee the next morning on a legislative bill regarding economic incentives for businesses in enterprise zones."

"We will not go into details, but would you describe your planned testimony as that of an expert witness on business tax incentives?"

"Yes, that is a fair summary."

"Were you in your hotel the entire evening?"

"No, I had gone to dinner with a group of south Texas business and political leaders who were also involved and supporting this legislation."

"What time did you return to your room?"

"About eleven thirty that night."

"Had you been drinking alcohol?"

"Yes, I had two glasses of wine at dinner before walking back to the hotel."

"Can you briefly describe to the court what happened after you returned to your room?"

I began to sweat. My scabs hurt and itched. The attorney saw I was hesitating, but she was patient. This part of the testimony was rough for me, but it was crucial to the state's case.

"One of the members of our dinner group, a chamber president from a nearby community, walked me to the room and ensured I was safely in the door. I immediately looked for the silk blouse I had left with the hotel staff for ironing, as I needed it first thing in the morning. It was not in the room closet. I called down to the front desk and inquired about my blouse. The night manager asked me to hold a moment and he would check in the back." I paused again to gather my courage.

"While I was waiting for him to return to the phone, someone knocked on my room door. I thought it was my blouse being delivered, so I dropped the phone receiver on the bed and opened my door. There was a black hotel employee standing in the doorway—I noted his employee name badge—but he did not have my blouse. He asked me if I ordered Tabasco sauce. I told him no, and he pushed his way into my room and proceeded to attack me violently. He raised the Tabasco sauce bottle and struck my face. The force of the hit and the hot sauce blinded me and I fell to the floor. He began punching my back over and over again. I did not realize at the time that he was stabbing me."

"Objection!"

"I think the court has understood that this woman was stabbed repeatedly no new information is being presented."

"Overruled. Proceed, Ms. Garrett."

"At some point, he pushed something down my mouth, I guess to muffle my cries for help. Then I heard some voices outside my room door. He stopped pounding my body and then the hotel door was forced open. He said to me, 'Lady, can I help you?'

"I did not know who had entered the room, but with what little breath I could I said, "Do not let this man go—he did this to me!'

"That is all I recall until I was in intensive care at the hospital."

"Would it be fair to say that you were physically attacked and suffered injuries to your nose, face, eyes, back, and internal organs and otherwise suffered traumatic and significant injury to your mental and psychological health?"

"Yes, ma'am. At the least."

"Can you identify the man who assaulted you for the court?"

I hesitated and kept my focus on the prosecutor, not wanting to waiver.

"Mirabelle, will you identify the man who assaulted you?"

I slowly turned on the witness chair toward the defendant and stared into the eyes of my nemesis. Our eyes locked for a moment. I raised my arm slowly and pointed my finger toward Leroy. He did not move or flinch. "That is the man who tried to kill me." The courtroom drew a collective breath.

"No!" Martha exclaimed. "It's not my son!"

"Order!" The gavel went down.

The judge stated, "Let the court record show that this witness identified Leroy Johnson as her assaulter."

"No more questions. Pass the witness."

The defense attorney had nothing to say. No objections. What could he say?

"No questions, Your Honor. Pass the witness."

"The prosecution rests."

"The defense rests."

It was in the hands of the jury now. And while the twelve men and women knew the facts of this case, they had no clue about what had happened a year before in front of the convenience store at the phone booth. But the sentencing proceeded despite their ignorance.

The next day the jury returned with its verdict. I had already departed the city where I was nearly murdered. I did not want to stay there and face my assailant another time. I had to escape the memories. My flight instinct was calling the shots.

The jury returned in about four hours. "Not too bad," thought the district attorney. It came as no surprise to anyone in the courtroom that the guilty verdict was handed down to the judge. What surprised the onlookers was the sentence.

Assault with a deadly weapon carried a maximum sentence of ninety-nine years. The jury did not want to appear to the public to give a "knee jerk" response and dole out the maximum, so Leroy Johnson was sentenced to ninety years in the Texas criminal justice system. When one of the jurors was told later about the earlier assault, she was mortified. Turns out that the previous sentence had been plea-bargained to a misdemeanor charge. Leroy was a well-behaved criminal and the county jail had already exceeded the number of prisoners it could hold by law. So he walked with barely a hand slap, free to make his way to the capital city and try it again.

■ ■ ■ ■ ■

Ironically, he almost beat the system when he came up for parole only seven years into his sentence. But that time, luck was not in his favor. He had created a foe—Lady Luck and my team of angels—he could never vanquish. But would the foe forgive him?

24

NEPAL

In early 1989, six years after my assault, I had emerged from physical healing for the most part and had done enough psychological counseling to establish for myself and others that I was of sound mind and not a risk. (Depression often befalls a victimized woman.)

But something else beckoned to me. A small stirring grew into a goal, pulling my soul across the Pacific to the tiny country of Nepal. Can a person put a finger on when a feeling becomes an idea and planning becomes real? My girlfriend Nicole agreed to be my traveling companion, and my office team of nearly three years were eager to prove their mettle and run our projects for almost a month.

Perhaps it boiled down to a moment of abandon. Nicole and I committed ourselves to embark on a 100-mile trek around the foothills of the Himalayans, known locally as the Annapurna Trek, led by Journeys Expeditions. Their brochure "ranking" of this excursion was "slightly above going on a long picnic." The reality unfolded quite differently.

We landed in Kathmandu and stayed a few days to get our bodies adjusted to the altitude. The pair of us rambled into the Shangri-La Hotel late in the afternoon. The porters grabbed our oversized green canvas army duffel bags and scurried down the tiled hallway.

Collapsing in some bamboo chairs in the reception area, we gave each other a long-eyed look, rolled our eyes, and exclaimed, "Can you believe we are here?!" We both started to grin and laugh out loud in unison. "Let's check in and find the bar," Nicole offered up. That was the last "normal" thing we did for the next three weeks!

Coming from the Rio Grande Valley, which is really a swathe of a broad delta in the southern tip of Texas, we were immediately impressed by the striking vertical landscapes. And the sheer effort it took us just to climb the first hill to reach the *beginning* of the Annapurna Loop. The trail was narrow, just wide enough for two abreast. We kept thinking we would see a horse or a mule, but we only met Nepalese carrying everything imaginable on their backs and shoulders. Up and down the rough-hewn rock steps. Ten steps, up and down, down and up—"There is no flat land in this place!"—as we reached yet another magnificent ridge with cascading mountains reaching ever farther into the horizon. We wore out moleskin patches on our feet, replaced them, and kept walking. For weeks.

I was too damn tired most of the time to reflect much on what "soul purpose" drove me here in the first place. Sometimes when you are immersed in the sheer work of the present, there are just too many distractions to reflect, but in years afterward, I realized that lessons were coming to me every day, just not in the way I expected them to arrive.

"How far to the campsite, Ming-Ma?" I asked our English-speaking Sherpa. He was a small, compact man with slighly protuberant teeth and a wide smile.

"Not far, only little bit more over the next ridge."

"You *always* say that," Nicole exclaimed with a wide toothy grin.

We kept going up and down, and down and up. "Climb every mountain," I began to sing out loud. I know all the lyrics to *The Sound of Music* songs from early piano lessons. "No, no no! That's too sad. Let's sing 'Do Re Mi' instead," and Nicole started off the song. I joined in to start the musical round, and to our surprise Ming-Ma joined in too. So we sang and sang until we couldn't sing another refrain, and what do you know, our campsite appeared out of thin air!

We threw down our backpacks, loosened our boots, and poured water over our faces and arms.

The sun was low in the sky; the colors began changing hue with the late afternoon light. Kids from nearby villages began to gather at the perimeter of our campsite and were really excited to see us and our camp gear.

"Come on, I want to show you something special," Ming-Ma whispered furtively, not to alert the other trekkers in our group. We began to descend into a leafy, forested area. The rock steps were obscured with fallen leaves and branches, so the going was slow. At least for Nicole and me. Village kids had followed us and were squealing with delight. They knew where we were going! Smiles reached ear to ear.

Nicole touched my arm, "Did you see him?" pointing to a child hopping in front of us leading our way. The light was dissipating. "Not really, what's up?" "He only has one leg."

Ming-Ma was leading us down a path to a small Buddhist shrine obscured by the forest. Walls were crumbling on one side, but we could smell the aroma of incense burning. The low angular light gilded the brass prayer rolls and incense burners. Colorful prayer flags hung listlessly on lines around the temple. Our troupe instinctively became quiet in respectful reverence for the site, but not too much. The gaggle of kids with the three of us gathered to sit on a nearby fallen log. After the jostling little bodies found their places, I pulled out the wooden flute I had bought in Kathmandu, for a moment just like this. Our makeshift three-part vocal harmonies filled the little clearing and the kids were wide-eyed and enthralled. Nicole noticed this first.

"Let's teach them a song, I bet we can, don't you, Ming-Ma?" Nicole looked at me expectantly. I had the flute, after all.

"Okay, sure, but do you have any song suggestions? Is there possibly a song we, who only speak English, could teach kids who only speak Nepalese?" I replied with a tiny hint of sarcasm.

Ming-Ma had already translated our idea. The children were excited. They nodded enthusiastically in the universal sign for "Yes, yes!"

I rolled my eyes at Nicole. "Oh brother, now you really put me on the spot."

"Think, think, think," she urged.

"I got it." Nicole and Ming-Ma both looked eagerly toward me. "'Kumbaya.' It's perfect. Even though it's African, it's perfect for this temple site. It's perfectly easy to teach because the words are easy enough to sound out and I can play the melody."

Ming-Ma shushed the kids and told them what we were thinking and motioned the group—now about fifteen strong—to come closer around the log. I drew a breath and played the melody once through. The tone of the flute flitted around the foliage. The shadows were more striking now. One by one, then two by two, then all the children's voices grew to one choir. Over and over, we sang the words we knew. We were singing for the sheer joy of the noise we were making. My flute became a conductor's wand and I made eye contact with every boy and girl to encourage them all to sing.

The chant was beautiful, extraordinary. Ming-Ma, our erstwhile troubadour, started experimenting with creating a round within the choir, like he did for our "Do Re Mi" rendition. A few kids took his lead. Others stayed firmly on note. We must have sung for twenty minutes, none of us wanting to stop. But the light deepened and I conducted the kids to a finish using my improvised baton. The kids hushed their voices on cue and the music hung in the stillness of our unintended worship. Nicole started to get up, but I held her by the arm. "Be still, my friend. Savor this moment as this is a magical moment, one you will never experience again in your lifetime."

We scrambled up in the gathering darkness to our campsite, the kids to their homes, and tucked ourselves into our sleeping bags. The next morning, something equally awesome happened.

Dawn was just breaking and Nicole and I were just beginning to groan ourselves awake. We heard shuffling feet outside our tent and children's urgent whispers. We lifted our heads up slightly and shared quizzical looks. "Is there someone out there?" I whispered. At that moment, a small voice, then two, then many joined in singing "Kumbaya" to us that morning. This time the song was exuberant and joyful! The kids had found our tent, and gave us back some of the love we shared with them. I know the child with one leg was still leading the way.

Have you ever been presented with a gift so precious and selfless that the giving of the gift takes your breath away? As the strains of "Kumbaya" left us for memories, another gift was just over the next ridge.

We started at dawn on a thirteen-thousand-foot plateau with sheer drops on two sides. This was a "free day" in which to relax and just be still. There was a village down the path we could see from our vantage point, so after a leisurely breakfast with tea, Nicole and I went down to explore. We were greeted with curious and smiling faces—the villagers had seen trekkers before—and one couple invited us in their very humble home for tea. We had brought some postcards from Texas and little gifts to exchange, so we had a small conversation with the couple, language barriers notwithstanding.

Sauntering out of the small home, we took the gently sloping path to the center of the village. By now we knew that in the center of each small village was a raised dirt structure supported by rocks that served as a meeting place. Some of these markers were built around trees, like the one we were approaching.

As in most villages, when the kids saw us, they came out cheering and wanting to see what might be pulled out of the backpacks of trekkers. We did not disappoint and started sharing a bag of large green balloons for the children and a few dozen cardboard emery boards for the women. What a kid magnet; within minutes we were surrounded! "Baalune, baalune" they cried as they jostled up toward us. They knew how to blow up the balloons, but they did not know how to tie the ends, so we took the time to show several of them how to twist the end with their fingers and cinch the knot. They were hysterical!

Some of the moms had joined in the fray by now, wanting to see what the fuss was about. I whipped out one of the nail files and gently showed the women—using my own fingernail for the demonstration—what it could do. Then I asked for a hand. One woman proffered hers hesitantly, and I touched the end of her fingernail and began filing. She instinctively jerked back, but then extended it again. The lesson did not take long. Big knowing nods communicated their understanding and pleasure. Soon all the boards were in their hands and in feverish use on jagged dirty nails that had never seen a manicure.

Nicole and I were so pleased with the joy our small

gifts brought to the village that afternoon. But there was something else going on. Someone else was observing us in the shadows of the nearby buildings that were across the street. He had been walking back and forth, watching the melee, but not joining in. Just watching and listening. I had seen him. Nicole had too. But he kept his distance and we were having too much fun to pay him much mind.

After all the treasures from our homeland were gone and the kids had wandered off, Nicole and I took off down the path to the other side of the village, just to see what was there. We stopped and sat on some large rocks to contemplate the truly wondrous view in front of us. The majesty of the mountains, with ridges plummeting straight down to a glinting silver sliver of a river so very far below us, was awesome. Both of us were at a loss for words, it was so amazing, so quiet, so magnificent.

Then we heard shuffling feet. We both turned around.

"Do you recognize him?" Nicole asked me.

"Not sure, do you?"

Instead of the westernized clothes most of the Nepalese wore, this man wore a plain brown robe, cinched at the waist. His bearing was erect and confident.

"Was this the guy who was watching us in the village?" she asked me.

"Hard to say; we didn't get a close look, but he may very well be the same man."

I squinted my eyes to get a better look. He continued

to approach us, and when he was closer, we nodded to each other. Yep. But what was it he had on his arm? What was he carrying?

He came nearer and smiled at us. Then we recognized that a juvenile owl was perched on his arm. There was no tether on its legs. We were both pretty impressed! He pointed back toward the village, as if to say, "I saw you. I saw what you shared with my village." We smiled back and placed each of our hands together, palm to palm, fingers up, and replied "Namaste." The robed man came closer now and extended his arm toward us, proffering the owl. He motioned his arm up and down and seemed to tell us, "Take him; take this owl."

"Oh no, we have no money," we communicated by rubbing our pants pockets with outspread palms in yet another universally recognized sign language. He shook his head back and forth and gestured more firmly this time.

"Is he offering us a gift, do you think?" I asked Nicole without taking my eyes from this man.

"What in the world do you think we could do with an owl, for cryin' out loud?"

"Nicole, listen to me. I think he saw our friendship in his village and he wants to give us something in return. Something really special. This is probably the most precious possession he has. I know we can't take the owl back with us, but we can't brush him off either. We must be receptive and gracious toward him and his gift so he doesn't feel rejected. I think this guy is a leader or a priest in this village. He deserves our respect."

And with that I gently offered up my arm toward the owl and he gently alighted on me. His little head was bobbing side to side with some perplexity. He was on his way to being wise, but not yet. I held my arm out high and admired the little bird's courage and smiled at his owner. Then, I gently gave back his owl, his pet, his beloved possession. "Namaste," I whispered and made a slight bow. He returned our valediction, turned, and then eased back on the path toward his village.

Suddenly the scenery was only a backdrop to the beauty we had witnessed from this man's soul.

Watching him go, I had not a clue that I would be in extreme physical danger within mere hours and survived because of the simple kindnesses of strangers inhabiting this inspiring land.

■ ■ ■ ■ ■

Another dawn arrived, but the air smelled of distant rain. Peering out of our tent flap door, we saw that the overcast sky was low and threatening. We could see the line of the storm approaching. Our Sherpas had been muttering during our trek that the monsoons were late that year. "Up in the mountains, monsoons are strong. Winds are dangerous. Rains make rocks slippery. Mudslides can pull us down," Ming-Ma cautioned.

Panicked, all of us gathered at the campsite, our belongings in tow. We couldn't find our rain ponchos, so Nicole and I slipped plastic garbage bags over our heads and followed the Sherpas as well as we could. Soon thereafter, rain was blowing horizontally. Large branches tumbled across our path, nearly striking us. The sky was steely gray. We were leaning hard into the wind just to stay upright.

"Ming-Ma," I yelled, "we need to find shelter. Can we knock on someone's home and ask for help?" The group was so spread out at that point that all I could see were the three of us. He ran ahead and found a hut on the side of the path and banged on the door. The woman of the family answered and beckoned us inside. A simple pot hung suspended from three sticks over a small fire. "Would you like some tea?" translated Ming-Ma. We were extremely grateful and accepted her offer. In turn, we offered up some Snickers candy bars and a pack of Marlboro cigarettes. (The latter, we had found, was a welcomed universal currency!)

After the storm subsided, we shared our "Namastes" and started walking again. For the next several hours, we trekked nonstop but never did catch up with the rest of the group or the vital camping supplies.

As the day drew down on our group of three, I began to swoon and falter. My vision was blurry and a sense of vertigo forced me to sit down where I could along the trail. The feeling was like a really bad reaction to something I ate. Nicole was not sick, though, and we had eaten the same things. I could walk eight or nine steps and then would have to rest on a rock. We were clearly getting nowhere fast.

Nicole took charge. "Ming-Ma, we have to find a place for Mirabelle to lie down and rest. She is too sick to go any further."

"But the campsite is beyond the next village. We have to meet up with the rest of the group. We have no supplies," he replied, clearly concerned with the predicament.

"We won't make it there; *she* won't make it there. We, no *you*, have to find a place where we can stay the night in the next village."

"There are no hotels in these villages! No place to stay!" he replied in earnest, his eyes darting up the trail for any clues to help him out of this situation.

"You have to ask. You must find something when we get Mirabelle to the village." Nicole was adamant.

The pair shouldered me on the path again, and when we arrived in the next village, they laid me flat on the raised rock marker in the center of this tiny community. Both of them took off in search of a place to stay, and I remained there, still and sick. My strength had vanished. I prayed to the Father and asked for help, or a repayment to be more precise. "God, please let them find me some shelter. For all the times I lodged kids from 'Up With People' in my home these past years, let me find a home tonight."

And my prayer was answered. Nicole and Ming-Ma came running toward me and exclaimed with wide astonishment, "We found a place!"

Right on the square was a family that rented out a single room on the rare occasion a traveler sought shelter. There was no sign or outward indication of a "Room to Let," just word of mouth traveling quickly through the village chatter. My friends shouldered me again and we walked across the dirt square to the house. Once there, they eased me down onto a straw mattress bed. I didn't care one whit. I was sick, tired, exhausted, and . . . grateful. I closed my eyes. Nicole took over my care and realized that I had to eat and drink something, but we had no food. Our provisions were two villages farther down the trail.

"What do you think you could eat, Mirabelle? You have to get something down your stomach that will stay there." I heard her, but did not open my eyes. The straw tickled my skin. "I think I could eat some chicken." My voice was a monotone.

"Okay. Ming-Ma, can you ask the woman of the house for a chicken?" Ming-Ma chattered away and asked Nicole for some money. Nicole handed over $5.00. "Can she use American dollars? Is that all she needs?" The woman understood this and nodded her head affirmatively. She left and my friends went outside. I slipped into a light sleep.

BBBWWWAAACCCKKKK, BWACK, BWACK! I nearly jumped out of my skin! What was this? Our hostess was beaming. She extended a closed basket toward me with a live, and very nervous, chicken inside! "Oh brother, Nicole! How are we gonna eat that?"

"Don't look at me," Ming-Ma interjected. "I'm a Buddhist. No kill nothing!"

Sensing our bewilderment, the hostess—amid the cackling and clatter—went outside with the chicken in the basket. One more BWACK was all we heard. We had our chicken. Now we had to figure out how to pluck it and cook it. We city slickers had to improvise, but chicken was indeed on the menu that evening. And fortunately, I could keep it down.

Sleep was an easy friend that night, and Ming-Ma had to shake us both awake at first light. "Do you feel better? Can you go with us now? We have to get to the group; they don't know where we are." He was anxious, I could tell. I could also tell I was indeed better. After a little tea and bread and a splash on my face, I pulled my backpack on and walked out of the humble hostel, grateful to our hostess and glad to be back walking on my own two feet. We waved good-bye and left the village behind us.

Later that day as we walked the trail, Ming-Ma told us the story of how we got the chicken. "The lady went to her sister in the village because she had a few chickens. Those were the chickens that laid the eggs for her family, and she sold some eggs in the village. She would never kill one of her chickens even for her own family."

Nicole and I shared a glance.

"She told her sister that she had a sick woman in her house and she showed her the five dollars. The sister pointed to the chicken she could take and told her to keep the money. She offered it back to me, but I told her to keep it."

"Are you sure?" we pressed him in unison.

He shrugged. "That is what I am telling you because that is what she told me. It is true."

Three for three. A choir, a precious owl, and a priceless chicken. These gifts from the hearts of the impoverished and simple Nepalese people—all without an expectation of recompense—began to open up my heart. And I realized I needn't fear for my safety.

Later, much later, I realized that life lessons often come from the most unexpected places. I survived through the grace of strangers in a distant exotic land, and in order for my soul to move on spiritually, I would have to start from a place of grace and gratitude for simply being alive.

25

PAROLE PROBLEMS

Nepal's memories were months behind me. The Texas Lyceum was holding a quarterly conference and as a board member I was expected to attend. I looked forward to the three-hour drive out of town in my smooth XJS Jaguar. Steely Dan tunes soothed me as they came through my sports coupe's surround sound. The white lines of the interstate were whipping past me like the questions swirling in my mind. "What the hell had gone wrong? Why would he get out after serving just seven years of a ninety-year sentence? Who can stop the prison doors from opening for that bastard?"

Earlier in the week I had received a form letter from the Parole Board advising me that Leroy Johnson was to be released from prison according to a preliminary decision made by a three-member subcommittee of the state Parole Board. I dropped the letter on my tile floor and nearly collapsed. Once again the primal fear of death wrenched within my gut. Again, I felt the violation I endured rising in my consciousness—a feeling I had deliberately pushed away every day for the last seven years.

Retrieving the letter, I regained my composure. My first action was to call anyone and everyone I knew to try and stop the parole process. I called friends in high places: reporters, power brokers in the capital city, elected officials. To no avail. The wheels of the parole process kept moving toward that open door. I called the attorneys who represented me in court. The lead attorney would look into it, but she did not hold out much encouragement. She was confused as to what had happened, however, because her office held copies of the document that sent Leroy Johnson to prison for nearly a lifetime.

I drove to the newly created Victim Services Division and parked between the bright yellow lines on a freshly asphalted lot. Ironically, or perhaps coincidentally, I was part of one of the first groups of victims to be assisted in this groundbreaking effort by the criminal justice system. Yvette was the first director but said her hands were tied. All she could do for me was to give me a copy of the initial parole findings of fact.

I cried and pleaded with her. "I know, I read what the official record states, but how could this be happening?"

Yvette shook her head. She was very familiar with this case and she honestly could not understand what had been going on behind the scenes. She had made some background inquiries, but had come up with nothing. The next file on Yvette's desk beckoned. I left in tears.

Now, the hypnotic effects of the interstate lines lulled me deeper into my Jaguar XJS's leather seat. "I love this car, teal with biscuit leather. The burl finishes. Its V12 engine," I purred to myself.

I was traveling along I-37 at my favorite speed, 88 mph. The horsepower of the engines reminded me of the rides I had truly enjoyed on an Andalusian stallion a little while back. I had met up with an exciting man while still living along the Mexican border. Guillermo—that name really rolled off my tongue. He was a businessman looking for investment opportunities along the Frontera. But far more interesting was his history as a successful and wildly popular bullfighter. His urbane style and piercing blue eyes were magnetic. He whispered to me in more languages than I could understand. I simply could not resist this man—on any number of levels. He was in turn drawn to my intellect and exuberant style. One thing led to another and he soon invited me to his ranch west of Tampico, Mexico.

He sent his plane to collect me for a long weekend. I did not know exactly what to expect but was game to go. I packed a few special lingerie pieces just in case. My motto has always been "better to have it and not need it than to need it and not have it." I was prepared for almost anything, but when I arrived, I was simply blown away. The driver picked me up at the small private strip in a dark SUV and drove me to the ranch. The entry gate was enormous and embellished with silhouettes of black bulls, bulls bred exclusively for the fighting rings wildly popular in Mexico.

Off to my left was an impressive stable and off to my right was a herd of black bulls and white dappled horses. They were from the ancient Spanish line of high-stepping spirited Andalusians. The expansive pastures lay along gently rolling hills as far as I could see! Damn. It was gorgeous. I grinned with the memory. But it was the feeling of riding one of his white stallions on a glove-soft Spanish saddle that drew my memory aside at the moment. The stallion's powerful haunches cantering at my command. A tiny flick of my heel and a subtle shift of my body weight was all that was needed for the horse to respond. Beautifully. Elegantly. Confidently.

Like the horsepower under my hood. But a black Mercedes sliding up beside me and passing my car on the left pulled me out of my daydreams. I cocked my head to ID the driver, but the windows were too dark.

As he described the scene later, Richard was skimming the black interstate, deep in strategic thoughts regarding a pending merger, when he looked to his right as he passed the Jaguar. He could see her profile. "Cute woman," he thought. Very nice. He felt a surge inside and did something he had not done in a long time. He mashed the accelerator and reveled in the quiet pickup of his highly refined machine. He smiled to himself.

"Hmm, that driver is aggressive," I thought. There I was hovering around 90 mph and this black machine was passing me by with ease. Hmm. I let him pull in front of me a few yards up and stabilize his speed. "Well, there is plenty more horsepower at my command." I checked the rearview mirror and glanced up the flat interstate for traffic. None. My radar detector was silent. I eased my Jag to passing speed and cruised by the Mercedes at 100+. What a great feeling!

Moments later, the Mercedes caught up and passed me again! He was playing with me; I knew it. Takes two to tango, so I eased on up a few notches and pulled ahead of him. This went on back and forth for nearly forty miles. When the refinery stacks came into view, I geared down to enter the city by the bay. I was on my way to the business meeting and was late for the opening presentation dinner. I grinned again. Well, not as late as I *could have been* going the speed limit!

I entered the tall sleek building that overlooked the gulf waters and punched the elevator button to the top floor. It was a private club. The view of the ocean bay was marvelous right at sunset. "Hey, how are you?" I said, shaking the club president's hand. I briefly worked the crowd, saying hi to some, giving air kisses to others. I sat down at a table where the salads were being served. Looking around the table, I did not know anyone, but I quickly and easily started chatting up the group. No wallflower in me!

To my right was a good-looking guy—small stature, slick hair—in a dark conservative suit. What really drew my attention to him was an odd thing. The organizers of this young leadership conference dinner had prepared nametags, and below each name was a little hand-drawn cartoon. "Cool cat in sunglasses" was my "emblem." But this guy had a "small person behind jail bars" cartoon on his badge. Since keeping Leroy Johnson in prison was heavy on my mind, I turned my head toward my dinner companion.

"And who am I lucky enough to be sitting by?" I asked, giving a flirtatious grin. He introduced himself as Richard Benchly. "I'm Mirabelle from south Texas, and I work in economic development—but play anywhere I can." I am incorrigible. "What kind of car do you drive?" A move to ask a sideways question.

He caught on to my repartee. "I'm partial to German engineering."

"You wouldn't happen to drive a Mercedes, would you? A black Mercedes?"

Richard returned an amused smile. "Yes, actually I do."

Now it was my turn to smile. "I was driving the Jaguar

XJS this afternoon." Together, we both laughed out loud! What were the chances of meeting each other after that little chase action on the interstate? That was rich.

Catching my breath, I settled down a bit and asked, "What do you do? Why the jail bars?" I pointed to his name tag.

"Well, what I do for a living is that I am a business attorney in Houston, mostly mergers and acquisitions. Pretty dull stuff most of the time. But what seems to take almost all my attention is my work in the state criminal justice system. I was appointed to serve in an advisory role."

Now I was doubly intrigued. "What do you know about the parole system?"

"What don't I know is more the question. I have worked in that policy area for a few years now."

I gazed at him intently, the rest of the room disappearing as my attention was riveted on this man. I had not met this person until a few moments ago, but my gut told me to make a move. "Well, then, I have a story to tell you," I countered.

Richard was an intense person in his own right. He had clear eyes and a clear mind. He listened to my plight with gathering interest.

"What year did the assault take place?"

"What was the charge?"

"What is his name?"

"What exactly was his conviction?"

"What was the sentence sent by the jury?"

"Is he incarcerated now?"

"Where?"

"And who sent you this letter advising you of his potential release?"

"When did you get that letter?"

My answers appeared to strike a chord. Richard was thoughtful for a few moments. He had been asked for help from strangers many times in the past. Most situations were run-of-the-mill, and others were truly gut wrenching. This decision was easy to make. Mirabelle "cool cat" needed help and it was easy for him to ask for information.

The entrée arrived and he shifted his attention to others around the table. Taking his shift as a cue to back off a bit, I let him absorb my tale. The trout almandine was a little bland and needed some lemon juice. I stole a wedge from my iced tea.

When dessert and coffee were served, Richard turned to me and said, "I will be in Austin next week for a meeting." He asked me if I knew where a certain bank building was downtown. "You come by right before noon. If the meeting has not finished up, you have someone come in and get me out of the meeting. Let me look into this for you."

The following week, I arrived as instructed at the first

floor of the tallest building downtown and let a receptionist know who I was and the person I was meeting. The staffer was prepared for me and gently knocked on the door. In a few moments, Richard eased his way quietly into the foyer.

He brought another senior staff member with him. I did not know this official, nor were we introduced. In his hand he carried what appeared to be a file. I did not see the contents of the file, nor did I ask what it was.

"It was a clerical data input error, Ms. Garrett. The crime he was convicted of carries a twenty-year flat time in prison. He is not up for parole now, and won't be up for another thirteen years. We have verified the clerical error. We are very sorry for your emotional distress." His tone was perfunctory and dismissive.

I looked into Richard's face and his expression told me his assistant was telling me the truth. He imperceptibly nodded and turned back to his bank meeting behind closed doors.

After the door clicked shut, I slumped in a nearby leather high-backed chair. Tears welled up. My neck muscles began to relax. My whole body melted into the oversized chair and I sat there—still, barely breathing— until I could regain my composure.

Walking outside into the bright noonday sun, I thought, "Now what were the chances of my meeting that guy at that time in my life when everywhere I turned there was no one to keep this guy in prison?" I had seen more than my fair share of the work of divine intervention in this ordeal. There was no other explanation—the chances of resolving the parole situation through the regular channels proved to be nil. I turned my face toward the sun and gratefully beamed a prayer of thanks.

And, indeed, I did not receive another such letter for thirteen years.

26

SO OTHERS MAY NOT ENDURE WHAT I HAVE ENDURED

After all these years, I am still pissed that Governor Ann Richards refused to sign the bill that had cleared both bodies of the Texas legislature.

It was early March 1991, and the legislature was back in town. The Texas sky was big and clear and I still marveled at the tallest capitol dome in the country. The pink granite dug from quarries by slaves encased the building with a hue not found anywhere else. Well, at least not anywhere else on this continent.

As I was walking up the long hill from Main Street, I

recalled looking at tall pink granite pillars in Egypt, wandering around on a very hot day in the renowned ruins of Luxor. At first, I did not pick up on it, but once inside the Karnak Temple within the Luxor grounds, I kept feeling that I had seen that granite before somehow, somewhere. When I returned home, I reached out to one of the geological professors at the University of Texas and asked about the similarity in color. It turns out that Luxor and Austin lie along about the same latitude and he was not surprised that the granite was so similar. I smiled, recalling my hot-air balloon ride with Charles over the Nile and the Valley of the Kings and Queens. But enough of that. Keep striding—I have work to do this afternoon.

In fact, I was apprehensive about this particular meeting at the capital. It had been almost ten years since my assault and I was still emotionally vulnerable. My scars on the outside had healed quite well, for the most part, but it was very hard to bring that day up to the surface. I had received a call out of the blue two weeks earlier with a completely unexpected request.

A prominent lobbyist had called. I knew Mike and I was a little surprised to hear from him because we worked different issues in the legislature. But politics makes strange bedfellows and the "circus" was in town, and I knew just about anything could happen during session.

Mike was representing the Texas Hotel Association, and his client wanted the law to be changed to allow hotel employers to seek a criminal background check on any new potential employees. Mike was a native Austinite and recalled my assault and the newspaper accounts. He also seemed to recall that my assailant was a hotel employee—but the hotel management denied this. He was vague on the details after that.

"How are you, Mirabelle?"

"About as crazy and tired as you are in this session, Mike! How are you?"

"Hey, it's only getting started. Say, I wondered if I could speak to you a moment about a bill I am working on."

"Sure, of course." I quickly scanned my mental file of active bills within my stewardship. Nothing came to mind.

"I'm representing the Texas hotel and apartment industry this session."

I clinched up inside. I thought I knew where this conversation was probably going.

"They want to get a bill signed that would let them check out a prospective hire's criminal background. They can already do an employment history, but are prohibited from digging into criminal histories. I know this might be a tough request for you, and I completely understand if you want to pass, but I was here when you were attacked and several other folks around here recall that as well. Your testimony would make a compelling case for hotel security background checks. Representative Blair is one of the cosponsors and he would be deeply grateful for your testimony, if you think you could do it. He completely understands if you think this is too much to ask."

I shifted in my mauve office chair. I did not answer directly. I looked out at the slow-flowing river of the capital city. I was not prepared to answer . . . not yet.

"Mike, that is a tough one for me. I know it's been nearly nine years, but I have never been public with my story outside of the courtroom, and I've shared it in only a few private conversations. I can tell the story, but I don't know if I could hold up in public testimony. I'm gonna have to think about this. When do you need an answer?"

"The committee is scheduled to take up the bill in two weeks' time. Since the vice chair of the Committee on Public Safety is supportive, he can be a little flexible in the actual scheduling of the bill to be heard. I also wanted to let you know that the association is prepared to pay you a consulting fee for your services."

He paused and looked out his own office window with a full view of the capitol dome a mere block from where he was sitting. His reflection reminded him that he needed to take his daily run along the river downtown. He had to stay fit and healthy during session as the demands of late night dinners and cocktails were part of the job. He did not rush me. As an experienced persuader, he knew when to talk and—most importantly—when to listen. He glanced at the sheaf of draft bills on his desk. Lots of calls yet to make today, but he was patient.

"Mike, I don't know if you realize this or not, but the hotel did not do any background check at all on my assailant. Is this proposed language permissive or mandatory on the background check?" In other words, I was asking if the bill would force the hotels to do a background check on each prospective hire, or would it allow hotel management to do such a search if they opted to do so?

"It's permissive. The bill would allow management to investigate to a deeper level than they can do now, but we won't force the issue. One would hope that given the opportunity the prudent thing to do, for any hotel, would be to secure the background of any employee who could enter the domicile of its guests. Other states have implemented such a step and the insurance industry is beginning to ask for this." He paused for a moment.

"Mirabelle, I've been given the authority to offer you a significant consulting fee for your testimony. You will not have to prepare a written statement, only provide verbal testimony to the committee. Tell your story. What you choose to say or not say will be completely up to you."

I knew my reputation preceded me with this last statement. Mike had seen me testify on other bills and was confident that I could deliver a punch if I decided to go through with it.

"Let me think about this, Mike. Can I call you before the end of the week?"

"Of course. Take care." Mike hung up the phone. He thought there was a better than even chance I would do it but did not want to call his client yet. His secretary interrupted his speculation with another urgent call holding on line three.

I was shaken. I left my office and went to the ladies room down the hallway. Good, no one was there. A stall offered privacy and I sat on the toilet seat to collect my emotions. "I think I am over this whole ordeal, then something like this smashes up against my world and here I am back in the hotel room all over again." I started to cry. I stayed there in the stall with silent tears. Grabbing some tissue paper I wiped my face and gathered myself. There was a sadness splayed on my expression in the mirror. A bit of cold water and paper towels held tight to my face helped me revive before I returned to my office.

That had been three weeks earlier. I agreed to do it, but on the condition that I would not accept a fee for my testimony. However, he agreed to donate the fee to our community shelter for women. I decided that this was going to be my way of "giving back" to the world. Karma, if you please. If this proposed legislation became law and prevented anyone from enduring the pain I continued to endure, then my effort might be a good thing. My nobility of purpose was fading precipitously as I strained up the hill toward the capitol. This was not going to be a pleasant experience. I anticipated that much.

I climbed the granite steps striding in my low-heeled black Italian pumps. I used my body weight and pulled open the oversized door and brass handle to the capitol building, nearly bumping into a group of tourists fresh from a guided discussion of the building provided by a Texas Ranger.

I moved through the entry hall to the circular area directly under the dome. I knew where the committee room was but had to assess the crowd and the rhythm of the business before selecting which way to go. I knew of a private elevator over to the side that I could use if the Senate was not in the process of voting. Not hearing any bells, I spied the dark metal embossed elevator door and punched the call button. Thankfully, there were no other passengers in this tiny portal.

When I got to the room, I was taken aback at the crowd inside. Standing room only. "Wow. I didn't expect this. What bills are up for a hearing besides mine?" I wondered. I scanned the room for a friendly face, and yes, he was there. A close but silent confidant who would provide emotional support. He was a high-powered mergers attorney and he had encouraged me to see this through.

Mike also saw me enter the room, and nodded my way. He had held a seat near the front of the room for me, and

I weaved my way through the crowd and shook Mike's hand. He took me to the dais and introduced me to Representative Blair and Chairman Bill Carter very briefly. The meeting was called to order.

HB 142 by Representative Blair was not first on the list, so I had a few minutes to collect my thoughts. There were several criminal bills up for consideration that day. "That must be why all the reporters are stacked in the back," I thought. The committee went about its business and bills were called up and discussed. Some had witnesses; some were procedural, with an occasional agency staff registered for information purposes only.

I was nervous. I twisted the short hair strands at the back of my neck. I tried to stay calm and evaluate the committee members as I would for any bill I was about to testify on, either for or against. There were nine members, seven men and two women. But only six were present that day. Three were Republican and three were Democrat; the others were absent. The committee clerk called out the bill number and Representative Blair was recognized by the chair as author of the bill. The crowded room quieted down. Some of the news reporters knew what was coming. Representative Blair formally introduced the bill and provided some background on why he and other cosponsors had drafted the legislation. He reminded the committee that the language was permissive, not mandatory.

"Today, committee members, we are considering a bill which might prevent crimes of the most heinous nature in a hotel room. Patrons of hotels have the expectation of privacy and safety when they enter their rooms. It is their home for the night. You may be surprised, even astounded, that under current law hotel management may not seek criminal background checks on their personnel. These employees are security staff, maid staff, room service staff, maintenance staff, and even management staff. So today, when you enter a hotel room and close your door, you may think the staff—and indeed may hope the staff—is part of the protection the hotel provides for your lodging. This, however, is not the case." He paused for dramatic effect.

"I am going to ask Mr. Scott Thurmond, executive director of the Texas Hotel Association, up for a little background on the subject."

The man next to me got up and approached the table with a thick file in his hand. I did not know who he was. Normally, the lead lobbyist would have had a pre-hearing conference to orchestrate the testimony, but Mike opted not to stress me. He knew my willingness to participate was tenuous.

Mr. Thurmond came to the front table and adjusted the microphone. He provided his name and address for the record. He knew he was not the primary witness for Representative Blair, but he had his role to play to provide information to the committee on what hotel management in Texas could and could not do in the hiring process. He also speculated that if this bill were to become law, insurance companies would require hotels to submit criminal background reports on any persons with authority to enter a domicile provided by the hotel. That was the technical term. He also expressed that from his experience and knowledge, he would very much expect that hotel hiring practices would embrace this new law and willingly use this new information source if they could do it legally. "It would be for the safety of our guests and would make good business practice," he concluded.

Chairman Carter resumed control of the hearing and asked the room to quiet down.

"I am going to ask the next witness to provide her testimony for the committee. I want to warn you in the audience that her testimony will be disturbing for most, if not all, of you. The story has strong violence and you may want to leave the hearing room."

The sitting crowd grew very still. No one left the room.

He nodded to me to step forward.

For a moment, I was unable to move. "Have I really done the right thing by being here? Can I go through with this? There are so many people in the room, what will they think about me if I tell them my story? Will some of them think I deserved it? Will they think I was raped?" The eyes of the chairman beckoned.

I sat alone in the chair along the oblong table. I adjusted the microphone. I had done this exercise many times in economic development legislation, but now I personally was on the stand as a victim, open for critical and sympathetic appraisal.

"My name is Mirabelle Garrett and I reside in Austin, Texas. I believe that had this bill been law nine years ago, I would not have been brutally assaulted by knife and bludgeoned within a hair of my life." I took a deep breath and plowed on.

"I work in the field of economic development and was in Austin to provide testimony on a bill for tax incentives involving job creation. Much like I am doing today. But unlike this day, I did not make it to the hearing. I was staying at a hotel nearby, and the night before the hearing I was assaulted by a hotel room service employee." I stopped again. I felt all eyes on my back. I felt like they could see my scars searing through my suit coat. I felt weak and exposed.

Seeing his witness falter, Representative Blair pulled me along. "How did you know he was an employee?"

"I had called down to the front desk because I had sent a silk blouse to be pressed in order to look my best for my testimony the next morning. When I arrived at my room after dinner, the blouse was not there. So I telephoned the front desk and inquired as to its whereabouts. Moments later, someone tapped on my door. I was expecting my blouse, so I opened it. I saw that the man had a hotel uniform on. But he did not ask me about my blouse. He forced himself into my room. He had a large commercial-sized Tabasco Sauce bottle in one hand and he slashed it across my face. The bottle broke and cut me. My eyes soaked up the sauce and were chemically burned. I could not see. What I did not know at that moment was that he also hacked my nose from my face with the jagged glass of the bottle."

I again paused to regain my composure. I held onto the tissue in my hand.

"Then he rammed a plastic garbage sack down my mouth and throat to stifle my cries. He raised his knife twelve times and stabbed me repeatedly."

I sobbed. I could not help myself.

The representative intervened again. "Was this man caught?" he asked, knowing full well the answer his staff had provided.

"Yes, sir, he is in the Texas prison system. I expect him to be incarcerated for a very long time."

"How long?"

"Sir, the jury found him guilty and sentenced him to ninety years. However, I understand that he may be paroled after twenty years. That will depend on the deliberations of the Texas Parole Board."

"Why have you come forth with your testimony today, Ms. Garrett? This is obviously difficult for you. So why put yourself through this?" The representative knew what answer to expect from me at this point, nearing the end of my testimony. It was a question that I had insisted he ask me.

"When women travel from home and their safety net, we are vulnerable. We feel vulnerable—even if we carry on doing our business commitments. We are more apt to be victims of violence than men. But we expect and indeed hope that our hotel rooms are safe and will keep us from harm's way. It is my sincere hope that this bill will provide the ability for hotels to conduct criminal background checks on their employees. It is my deepest trust that your bill will prevent another woman from vio-lence at the hands of a hotel employee."

"Why do you feel this bill would prevent your assault from happening again, Ms. Garrett?"

"Because, sir, this employee had a criminal history before he was hired. He tried and failed to kill another woman in his home town."

The chairman scanned his fellow committee members, then the silent crowd in the room. He knew he had made his point with this witness.

"Thank you, Ms. Garrett. I am sure the committee has no questions. We are grateful that you have come forth today to testify."

When I turned around to retake my seat, the people close by could see that my makeup and mascara had run down my face. Thankfully, the man next to me extended his handkerchief. Gratefully, I wiped my face.

The committee clerk called for a vote on HB 142. I was surprised how close the vote was. Four in favor, two opposed. The committee chair called for a recess. As I was weaving my way back down the room, several reporters approached me. Mike had anticipated that and warned them away from me. However, he did let one of the committee members approach me as I was breaking for the door.

"Ms. Garrett, I want you to know that I was prepared to vote against this bill. But when I heard you and learned what happened to you, I changed my mind. Your story made the difference for me. I thank you again for sharing your terrible, terrible experience with us today."

HB 142 successfully was approved by both chambers of the Texas legislature. But it was stopped cold by Governor Ann Richards's veto. The explanation provided by her chief of staff was that she felt the bill fell too far from the privacy rights of Texans.

It would take the next governor and future president of the United States to sign an identical bill approved, again, by both chambers in the next legislative session. It is now the law in Texas that a hotel employer may seek a criminal background check on its prospective new hires.

27

THE LIGHT OF THE GROTTO

"Ugh—do I really have to get up?" I peered through the small round window of my cruise cabin. "It's not even light yet!"

My roommate, Jennifer, offered no encouragement; she was still lightly snoring in her very early morning sleep. The best kind.

Our ship was docked on the Greek island of Patmos. I could not see much of the craggy rock perimeter because the sun was taking its own sweet time about peeking up above the horizon. Or maybe I was just taking my own sweet time in getting out of bed. Our cruise group had been up late the night before, dancing, drinking cocktails, and having a little casino action. Regular fare for a Christian tour group retracing the "Footsteps of Paul" around the Aegean Sea, don't you think?

Our leader was a remarkable man by any measure. Pastor Gerald hailed from a West Texas background and was an enthusiastic Baptist in a well-established church in downtown Austin. He, his wife, Louise, and a small group of energetic, visionary congregation members saw the need for a different kind of church. A church for people who didn't want to go to church. Didn't have a church and probably didn't want a church. The band of believers broke off from the downtown church and established Riverbend to start a fresh new common sense approach to sharing God and Jesus. For the bruised, the battered, the broken, and the bored.

The trip provided lots of inspirational bits, with an equal share of historical ones. As Pastor Gerald put it, "I will speak and teach not only from Paul's writings but also from the ideas of the Greek philosophers who challenged Paul. As we always do, we will blend spiritual growth with a downright good time!" And so it was. I even managed to find a cute Greek guy on Rhodes and took off with him on his moped for the afternoon. White table wine and a delightful detour were over all too soon before the ship schedule beckoned me back on board.

Our group excursion to Ephesus the day before had

provided a funny incident. As the group was walking along the ancient road toward the amphitheater, our pastor gleefully pointed out a carved inscription on the road. It was a sign of sorts, a billboard in antiquity on the highly trafficked marble road heading to the center of the city. The "inscription" was a man's foot pointing directly ahead to what used to be the "cat house" of Ephesus. He really chuckled at that one. His wife rolled her eyes at her husband's antics.

The day was clear; the afternoon sun was getting hot. Pastor Gerald was describing how Paul wanted to address the Ephesians in the amphitheater but the local sheriff dissuaded him as the crowd was unruly and in no mood for Christian dogma. As we mounted the stage and looked up the hill to the semicircle of seats, Pastor Gerald drew in a breath, stretched his arms wide and softly shared with the gathered, "This will be the style of our new sanctuary, seats rising up from the stage at the bottom."

(Years later, the Riverbend Home for Hope was completed. I continue to sing in the church choir even today.)

Late the night before, Pastor Gerald had reminded his tender flock to get their butts out of bed early the next morning if they wanted to witness a singular spot on this planet—the place where the Book of Revelations was written. Or, as I refer to it, "channeled" by the Apostle John and captured with ink by his scribe.

Steadying myself with the waves and the gentle rock of the ship, I felt my way to the tiny head. No time to wait for hot water, so I splashed my face with cold water and ran my fingers through my clipped brown hair. "Hmmm, my left eye is not so bad this morning, a little red is all." I self-consciously peered at my facial scars and confirmed, yes, they were still there. I secretly wished that one day I would wake up to find my scars gone, my eyesight returned. But not today. Not today. And certainly not now.

I threw my toothbrush in and out of my mouth, slid out the narrow cabin door, and bounded down the corridor. I saw our group gathering together at the appointed table in the dining room. After a few clumsy morning hugs—everyone was a bit of a grumbler at that hour— Pastor Gerald pulled the group together with a quick overview of the grotto we were about to visit.

"It's a steep walk up to the cave and the monastery, so grab some coffee. We will take it slow, but we need to keep moving. A sect of Greek Orthodox priests oversees St. John's Grotto, enclosed as it is by the Monastery of the Apocalypse, which was built more or less around the cave more than 900 years ago.

"Remember, this is their Easter season. Generally, the grotto is not open until later in the morning, but the leadership has granted our special request to come as a group and visit the grotto by ourselves," he announced with a smile.

"Pastor Gerald rocks!" I thought. Now pumped up with excitement and caffeine, off we went in the early dawn. The road was crude, steep, and lined with white-washed eucalyptus trees. The morning scent invigorated me.

The steady ground of the rock island was a welcome relief from the sea sway on the boat. I was a little out of breath as we traipsed up the narrow road. Misty air hung near the ground, so I could not quite make out the tall walled structure perched on the top of the island. There was not much chatting going on, and the dampness of the early morning softened the sounds of our footsteps. Roosters sporadically jabbed the morning silence. Our group ascended at a slow pace.

Naturally curious, I picked up my pace and spirit as we approached the church and the famous cave. As we came into the grotto, the mood became even quieter and more reverent. The interior was made of gray stone with arches overhead. The occasional geranium flowerpot provided some cheerful color and pungent fragrance. The air was still and humid. The sky had turned to a brilliant blue.

Our group filed slowly into the grotto itself. It was small and very cramped. A few simple worn wooden benches were set into the rock floor. Inside the cave was the spot where St. John the Apostle had lain on the hard floor, a hole carved from rock serving as his pillow. Both it and the place in the wall where he put his hand to pull himself up are lined in silver. Pastor Gerald pointed to a crack in the ceiling of the cave that is said to have been made by the voice of God. I settled on a bench with two other companions, and each of us sat very still in contemplation. When all were gathered, Pastor Gerald led us in prayer. Then all was silent as we each communed with our own thoughts.

And that is when it hit me.

I was deep in contemplation when WHAM! I found myself knocked off the wooden bench to the floor. Of course, I was startled, as were my companions who had been sitting on either side of me on the bench, where they had firmly remained. "Are you all right?" they said in unison as they gently pulled me back up to the bench. I shook myself, like a dog might shake its body after a rain shower. "That was weird," was all I could think as I resumed my seat.

What I had "seen" the moment before I fell to the floor was a forceful, brilliant white light coming at me, opening itself up right at my face. It looked like a million zillion fiber optic cables fused with a great light. It had energy—forceful energy, God-like energy. I realized with dawning amazement that I had seen that light before. Yes! It was the same light! The Light that had dropped down to me on the hotel floor. While that had been almost fifteen years earlier, I recalled that moment with clarity and confirmation.

"Wow, now that was impressive . . ." I caught my breath and remained quiet. My companions looked at me with wondering eyes. I thanked them and kept my vision to myself. I still was not really sure what had happened. "But what if I asked the Light to come back to me? I wonder what would happen. I wonder how long I could feel the Light."

I centered myself back on the wooden bench and breathed deeply. Closing my eyes, I focused on the little spot under my left lung that had become my portal to prayer—the tingly spot. I prayed for the Light to return and envelope me. It didn't take long. This time the Light was a little slower in coming on, but within a second, the huge circle of fiber optic light wires returned. The diameter of the Light circle was well over three feet. The radiance was softly pulsating. White, very white. Strong light.

I consciously held the Light in my mind's eye for as long as I could. It felt as if time had stopped, and it very well may have. I could not hold on to the Power for long—perhaps only moments. But this time when I opened my eyes, I did not fall to the ground, and I was astonished and exhilarated that the Light had chosen to come back to me again—this time in a profound way, not in the midst of pain, blood, and anger. There was no voice this time, but the message I heard was an affirmation that all was well on the other side and the Light was still waiting for me—when the time was right—exactly as I had heard on that long night that was not nearly far enough away.

For me, this humble ancient portal of God's Light was very much alive and functioning. But what do you say to someone about the Light coming toward you—again? twice?—and not be discounted as crazy? Or worse? I waited for a quiet moment, some days later, to describe to Pastor Gerald what happened. I trusted him and needed him to talk to about this extraordinary experience. He listened carefully and without judgment to my story about how the Light came to me then and now. As a man of faith and good humor, he quipped, "Mirabelle, take the light into your life and be glad that God reached out and touched someone—you!"

28

DID IT MAKE MY BROWN EYE BLUE?

Since my assault in 1983, I have been able to regain virtually all of my movement. A little follow-up cosmetic surgery lifted my droopy left eyelid, which was stretched out of proportion from the excessive swelling that resulted from the glass bottle cuts and deep bruising. I did get a straightened nose out of the ordeal. The one scar that did not heal—worsened over time, in fact—was the cornea in my left eye. The Tabasco sauce that saturated my eyeball left deep chemical burns on and around my cornea. Gradually, the scarring overtook my cornea and slowly grew across my line of vision. For the last ten years or so, I have not been able to see out of that eye. In the fall of 2010, the scarring became acutely painful at times, so much so that I was unable to get out of bed from the blinding hurt. Other days it would be better, and I was more stable.

Searing pain and a *Newsweek* article—forwarded to me by my handyman—that heralded an intriguing new procedure, motivated me to investigate a way to heal my pain and depression. But I proceeded with pessimism. For twenty years, the answers I received from many, many ophthalmologists were disappointing. The prognosis was consistently bleak. My eye was too battered, too scarred for a cornea transplant. The pain had become so intense I had even had a serious discussion about removing my left eye completely. A prosthetic might have to do. I was at the end of my options and twenty years of being so tired of looking at the mirror every morning and seeing the last physical reminder of my assault.

I backtracked and discussed this procedure with the original ophthalmologist who helped me heal from the beginning. Dr. Lee cared for my eyes for months until the right eye cleared and the left eye stabilized. Later, he was elected president of the Texas Ophthalmological Association and became an American Academy of Ophthalmology fellow. I saw him occasionally at the state capitol complex when we were both doing our "rounds" as lobbyists. So I knew he was connected to the premier physicians in the field.

It was a good call. In twelve days' time, I was in the office of Dr. Steve Pflugfelder, a rock star in the field of cornea surgery. I was immediately taken with his calm, confident manner. He was patient with my stream of questions based on my myriad file notes. He was patient with my skepticism. He calmed my anxiety. Like one of Pavlov's dogs, I was so accustomed to the well-meaning but sorrowful look they wore when doctors told me nothing could be done, I had to double-check Pflugfelder's face when he gave his answer.

"You are a perfect candidate."

"What?" I was confused with this unexpected diagnosis.

"Your eye is indeed damaged, but the stem cell transplant procedure should work very well for you," he explained, still calm and steady.

I frankly was afraid to believe him. But he carried on his explanation of the surgery.

"We take limbic stem cells from your good right eye and place them in your left eye. We next add some donor limbic stem cells to act as a conduit for your own stem cells to grow toward—like a bridge. We will put a little placenta tissue over your eye, sew it up, and wait for about ten days."

"What is your success rate?"

"It's about 90 percent. Your eye should heal through this and you should be able to regain your sight."

I left his office afraid to feel excited, but I grasped his

business card with all his contact numbers tightly in my palm. I would consider this and call back.

My mom was enthusiastic about this new option and played the role of the Great Encourager! She knows how I think and helped me address all my concerns and objections.

We scheduled the procedure for two weeks hence. I was ready. Dr. Pflugfelder gave me the confidence I needed to endure this arduous and painful procedure.

After some pre-op routines, my mother and I arrived at the outpatient surgery facility at 6:30 a.m. I was first up for the day. By 7:00 the nurses had completed their duties, and "Doctor Flug" (the nickname I learned he went by) arrived with a smile.

I really wanted to be knocked out of the ballpark. There was nothing in the procedure I thought I would want to remember, so I received permission to keep my earbuds from my iPod in my ears and the drugs washed me out in a second or so. Quick.

About two and a half hours later, I was awake with a big eye patch on my left eye and a smiling anesthesiologist hovering around my bedside.

"All done!" she announced. Still full of good loopy drugs, I nodded slightly.

I rested the remainder of the day and returned the next morning for a look-see and medicine check. I was still physically overwhelmed and in a great deal of pain.

My brother flew into Houston to be my chauffeur.

We stopped in Crockett for lunch. As I expected, the convenience store where my assailant had committed his first crime was long gone. But the courthouse where he was found guilty of that vile offense was still standing. My brother took some pictures for my book. We returned to Austin, and the healing process for my cornea began in earnest.

I was surprised by how long it took to heal. I have also been surprised at how closely I had to monitor my pain medications. If the lapse between doses was too long, my eye started to sting in a million places and to tear copiously. My grandmother's handkerchiefs came in handy. They are always close to hand and remain damp with my tears. Applying the three eyedrops twice a day is also a challenge. My left eye was sewn nearly shut, so there is only a tiny space through which to apply drops. At first, my eye was so swollen I could not manage well at all and needed help from friends and family. And I dared not press too hard on my eyelashes to clean out all the dried drainage. The drops had a lingering sting to them.

Nearly ten days into recovery, I had a real relapse and nearly collapsed on my kitchen floor tiles. A wash of pain came over me and my eye began to tear profusely. I stumbled downstairs to my bed to wait out the sensation. I popped another Percocet. Dreamy time until nearly nightfall.

I listened to an audio version of Oscar Wilde's *The Importance of Being Ernest.* Such a great play. My favorite lines are: "There you have it, the truth, pure and simple. Ahh, but the truth is rarely pure and never simple." Indeed. Through my ordeals, sometimes I can only glimpse at the whys and wherefores of the truth.

I felt better the next morning and was paying closer attention to the timing of my pain meds. I thought about chronicling this adventure but could not begin to gather my thoughts, much less type them coherently. I started to fade that evening but then rallied when some friends picked me up to attend a mutual friend's Valentine's Day party at his home across the Barton Creek gully. I played along by taping a heart onto my glasses and wearing a name badge that read "Call me stem cell transplant Mirabelle. One-eyed lovers are more focused!" You've just gotta laugh at yourself sometimes!

I really thought I would be healed, or close to it, on the second morning after my near-collapse. But I guess healing can take a zigzag course, not a linear one. So I returned to my bed and meds and stayed still, though was—and still I am—tired of staying still.

Three mornings after the crisis, at 4:30 a.m., I awoke because of the pain in my eye. Popped half a Percocet and went back down. Dreamy time again. Finally coaxed myself up mid-morning. Up to that point, ibuprofen was enough to tame the pain beast. But I felt cooped up and wanted to get out. My muscles were sore from not working out. "Something has to give," I shouted to my empty room.

Through it all, I have been contemplating how I feel about having two other people in my eye. I am thankful for the decisions each of them made: one donated his eye from which the stem cells were harvested, and the other, a mother of a newborn, donated a small—tiny even— piece of her baby's placenta. Yes, this was another part of my journey made possible through the gifts of strangers. I am not alone in my soul journey and now an understanding has evolved within me to recognize that none of us is alone. Sometimes we feel desperately lonely, but we can reach out, call out, scream out if need be. We each have helping hands and eyes and smiles and love to guide us along our ways.

Finally, on the morning of the fourth day, I awoke with no pain. No meds. That lasted about an hour. Then back to Percocet bits.

V-day, February 18, 2011! My body urged me forward to work out, get out, walk out. It was a beautiful Austin day, 72 fair degrees. A good day. Come evening, my muscles began to feel pleasantly, reassuringly sore.

Feeling less pain on the weekend, I spent much time online catching up with bits and pieces of work—yes, work. Actual work. I was monitoring my legislation progress, grateful that no hearings at the capitol were scheduled for me that week. I did not want to testify wearing an eye patch. But wait a minute; maybe I could wear the Red Cross version that Daryl Hannah's character

Elle Driver wears in the *Kill Bill* movies or the sinister pitch-black model Angelina Jolie's Captain Franky Cook brandished in *Sky Captain and the World of Tomorrow*!

To celebrate that productivity, on Sunday evening, my buddy James and I went to a movie, then to dinner. We sat with some mutual friends at the Café on the Run because the place was full, full, full. My favorite local crooner Dale Watson was playing "Route 66." James was on my left side, and we sat arm in arm. I was sharing the story of my way cool high-tech stem cell transplant eye surgery and brought up Crockett and a nurse.

Melinda, Larry's wife, shared, "That reminds me of a Catherine that I know—she was from Crockett."

"She used to be a nurse?"

"Yes, now she works at the Texas Railroad Commission."

"Wow, will this story never stop?" I said to myself.

My face registered honest surprise. I felt my body go weak. I glanced at James, who was listening with great attention.

"That's her! She was the nurse in the emergency room who recognized Leroy as the assailant who attacked her a year before! It was her ER surgeon who demanded that the police return to my hotel room and find the knife because they were about to release him since they did not find a weapon on his person."

Shortly after that evening, I wrote to Catherine at her

work address. It will be interesting to reconnect with her after all these years.

A week later and she still had not contacted me. I could only speculate on the reasons for her hesitation.

Meanwhile, my left eye had progressed nicely. On my second follow-up appointment, I complained to the surgeon that my eye felt as though an eyelash or something was under the blank contact lens acting as a Band-Aid on my cornea. Very annoying, especially since I knew I could not rub my eye nor fiddle with the contact.

"Maybe it has something to do with the sixteen stitches left in your eye," he replied with just a bit of mischievousness. "Want me to take them out?"

I looked at him with a little attitude. "Yes, right this minute!"

So the numbing drops went in and the stitches came out, one at a time. Ugh. Each time we took a break I had to shake my hands and fingers from the nervous tension I was experiencing. After the tiny shreds were safely on a little glass dish and out of my eye, he took a photograph to show me how the cornea healing was progressing.

"It's about 85 percent grown back; see the blue patches? Those are the areas that have returned. These green areas still need the stem cells to grow over them."

I had yet to see much improvement in my vision, but at least I knew that the pain I was enduring was in the promotion of my healing progress rather than just the pure pain that preceded the surgery. Because in a few weeks' time, my journey would take a hard turn, and I would need all my emotional and physical strength to confront what was to stand in my path.

29

MY PREDATOR IS RELEASED

A swirling sensation comes over me. I blink several times to keep my focus on the discussion that is unfolding as I slump in my dining room chair. A sense of déjà vu eerily settles in around me. Almost like a slight fold in the curtain of time. I am there, yes. The officer is there, yes. His words are clear and audible. But I know what he is going to say just nanoseconds before his words reach me. My assailant will be released from incarceration in a few months. This reality has not sunk in. But it is catching on fast. Slowly the time warp dissipates and I begin to discuss in earnest what the criminal justice system has in store for me. And him.

Leroy Johnson has served for thirty years and he has earned two days for every one day of incarceration. Therefore, his ninety-year sentence is considered served, and he is expected to be released, soon, under Mandatory Supervised Parole as defined in the *Texas Code of Criminal Procedures*. The alternatives to keep him in prison have been exhausted. There are no means that I— or anyone else, for that matter—could muster that will change his scheduled release date.

A visceral fear begins to seep into my skin as the victim services analyst goes through the details. He is calm and practiced in this situation. We talk about what conditions I can request of the Texas Board of Pardons and Parole, and it boils down to two pretty basic parameters. The first is that he is going to be released in a county other than where I live, and the conditions of his parole can specify that he can never enter my county. If he did and he was caught, that would be considered a violation of his parole and he could be sent back to prison.

I am not comforted by this.

The second option the analyst describes is a Super Intensive Supervised Parole where a parolee's location is monitored with GPS technology via an ankle bracelet secured on the parolee's leg. But, as a victim, I could not know where he lives or where he might be traveling. Local and state law enforcement officers would know if the bracelet was forcibly removed or he broke from his approved area or "inclusion zone." If he is assigned an "active monitoring" system, police and surveillance personnel should know within minutes of any movement beyond the inclusion zone. Under a "passive monitoring" system, his movements would be tracked and reviewed weekly by a parole supervisor to determine if he has literally lived the straight and narrow parameters approved by the supervising parole officer: namely, his work, the grocer, his church, and a few other locations. But again, his movements among those locations will not be monitored in real time in a passive system.

So the fear continues to sink deeper in my blood. I have wondered over the years if Leroy Johnson has been darkly fuming over the years and secretly preparing his revenge. "One must hope for the best, yet plan for the worst," my grandmother would often say to me. I suddenly realize I do not even know what he looks like. "How am I to even recognize him on the street? Or breaking a window? How can I protect myself in the most basic way possible if I do not even know who to look for?" My mind is full of so many unanswered questions, and I take a deep breath and take my time to ask Officer Guerra each and every one.

"Well, there is one way you can get a hard look at him," explains the victim services analyst. I perk up with some level of trepidation. "The Texas Department of Criminal Justice offers a Victim Offender Mediation/Dialogue program, with the end result—if and only if both parties agree and I believe that the meeting will be good for both parties—being a face-to-face meeting while Johnson is still in prison."

This idea was not totally new to me. A few years after my assault, friends and counselors had begun to suggest to me that I consider forgiving my assailant. Yvette, with the Victim Services Division, related how some—not all—victims had found solace and strength for themselves after facing their offender and getting answers to some of their questions. Some had chosen to participate in a program administered by Victim Services where the victims ask to meet their assailant face-to-face in prison and speak to the criminals about the motivations of their actions. Sometimes the victim and the assailant are able to find some kind of peace between them.

"Forgiveness is a process" she shared with me. "It may take years, or it may never come at all. You will make that choice and no one will disparage you if you do not want to forgive him. He committed a vicious, terrible act against you. He is in jail and will stay in prison hopefully for a very long time. He did get ninety years, right?"

Frankly, at that time—very early in my journey—I was having nothing of it. It was not even in the realm of possibility. In fact, imagining a means to kill him inside prison was far more appealing in a primal sort of way. I imagined ways to set up the deal, how much it might cost, how it might play out. This was all fantasy, of course, but it felt far more satisfying than forgiving the asshole.

Now, as I listen to Officer Guerra, the concept of forgiveness enters my mind once more. I let the prospect of a face-to-face meeting sink in before I speak. The calmness in my voice belies my trepidation. "So I might sit across a table from Leroy Johnson and try to understand what kind of human being he is? And why he tried to kill me?"

"Yes, but he has to agree to do this," replied Guerra. "I can speak to him about this and begin to ask some of your questions as a way for you to initiate the process. Now, depending on his answers and his attitude, I may call this off. But that is not my intent. If I can mediate a meeting that—based on my twenty-odd years of experience—I anticipate can result in a good outcome for you, then we can proceed to the next steps. You know, you can pull the plug on this at any time—as can Johnson."

I searched his face, took a deep breath, and said, "Yes."

"Very well, let me meet with him and see what his reaction is. Any questions you want me to ask to get this started?"

"How about the obvious ones: Why did he try to kill me? What was his motivation? Is he planning to seek me out and harm me when he is released?"

Officer Guerra shook his head slightly as he said, "Let me share something I have learned from years of talking to criminals, Mirabelle. They tend, generally speaking, to say to you what they think you want them to say. Or say what they think will get them some kind of reward or get them out of a jam the quickest. You have to realize this when you are talking to him. The criminal may appear to be very sincere and very real, but don't count on his words being truthful. I'm just trying to help you set realistic expectations in my role as mediator in this process."

I nodded and replied, "Let me know what he says after your prison visit."

■ ■ ■ ■ ■

About two weeks went by and Officer Guerra and I continued the mediation dialogue. He conveyed the essence of the conversation he had had with Leroy Johnson. The officer first described my assailant's demeanor as meek and soft-spoken. He spoke slowly, often repeating himself. "He was surprised that you've asked to meet him, Mirabelle. He shook his head and told me he can't see why.

"Johnson then said, 'When I was in high school, I was a stupid young punk caught up in drugs and alcohol. I felt trapped and I felt lost. I had built up a rage that night in the hotel.' When I asked him, 'Why did you do that to Mirabelle?' he replied, looking down, 'Don't have no idea, man.'

"His body slumped, then, Mirabelle. He said, 'I was running with a bad crowd.' He looked up then and held my gaze. 'I would never go back to hurt her. I am truly sorry. I jes wanna start over. I wanna live a simple life. Not bring no attention to myself. Wanna play guitar in church. Wanna sit somewhere so's I won't be seen. I learned to run a print press. I can work at a newspaper.'"

Officer Guerra then described that the prisoner paused and seemed to try to collect himself. He sensed that Johnson was trying to express something that he hadn't expressed in a very long time.

"When he spoke again, Mirabelle, he said: 'I've paid for my crime every day of my life. And I should, I know that. But I done lost some things important in my life too. I loved my grandmama and she died whilst I was in here. My family done turned they's back on me. When I first got here, I was a punk and hung out with the wrong crowd. I'm older now. Done learned how to survive in prison and to stay away from bad influences.'"

Officer Guerra noted that Johnson seemed sincere. But his experience told him to hold judgment.

Then Guerra conveyed Johnson's last words at the end of the hour that passed between them. "'I'll meet her if my apology through you ain't enough,' he told me, Mira-belle. 'I will apologize face-to-face. I owe her that.'" The officer paused to let this sink in.

This was potentially a huge step for me and I needed time to pray and think through my next steps.

■ ■ ■ ■ ■

Days later, Officer Guerra and I continued the dialogue. Again, he couched his remarks in the context of a criminal's mind-set.

"I hope that I never get to understand it the way that you do, Officer Guerra," I said. "But it's a fair warning as we go further into this process."

Perhaps because I imagine the worst, and I've been told not to trust what Johnson says, I am on guard. As I listen to Officer Guerra, his words begin to slowly fill in the vague outlines of an image I have held of Leroy Johnson for all these years. I take his report in, reminding myself to breathe. I have kept up with the Texas prison unit Johnson was in, but that was about it. Frankly, he deserved this punishment, and the bleaker the better. Now I was hearing that he says he's sorry and did not know why he attacked me. All he could muster was, "I have no idea."

How does one respond to that? Was I just simply in the wrong place at the wrong time? Even though I paid for a hotel room I thought to be secure? That they were responsible for keeping me safe? And failed?

But my mind keeps wandering to that still place Lynda suggested years before. Was this a chance meeting or was the assault determined by a Higher Power?

■ ■ ■ ■ ■

According to Officer Guerra, Johnson was far more animated during the second interview he conducted with him a few weeks later. The two-hour talk in a tiny office revealed a nervous and anxious prisoner. He seemed hesitant to express himself. Johnson had clearly thought about the mediation process and perhaps had sought advice from his prison peers. Officer Guerra speculated they were older and wiser inmates, but still he had to question what, if any, motives his peers might have had making the suggestions they did—which Johnson had seemingly swallowed hook, line, and sinker.

"Mirabelle, I asked Johnson point-blank, 'Do you think they want something from you when you get out?' He did not reply. He either had not thought that far ahead or did not want to answer. Distrust was still hanging between the two of us.

"'I jes don't wanna think about it,' he said. 'I want to forget about the whole damn thing. Don't wanna go back to that time and that place ever again. I wanna move on with my life.' He reiterated what he'd said during our first session. 'I don't wanna harm her. I jes wanna live a quiet life.'"

Officer Guerra said he pressed on, not wanting Johnson to take the easy way out just because the thought of seeing me was uncomfortable. "I asked him, 'Do you recall that you broke a bottle of Tabasco on her face?'

"Johnson slumped and replied, 'Yes.'

"'Did you know that the injuries you gave her still have not healed? That she had an operation just this past year to regain the sight in one eye that you took from her?'

"At that moment, Mirabelle, Leroy Johnson collapsed emotionally. He broke down at the desk in that stuffy little room. He sobbed. His composure left him for at least ten minutes. Then he regained himself. 'I really don't wanna go on with this less'n I know for sure that she wants to do this.'

"I got a burr under my saddle then, Mirabelle, and fired back at him, 'What, you think I'm inventing this whole thing? Why should you ask anything of her, anything at all?'

"'Because I'm nervous, man, and I wanna know from her—through you—that she honestly wants to go through with this, 'cause I don't. I guess I owe her that much, if she really wants to do this. I want something to show she really wants to do this, like reassure me she's sincere.' His eyes met mine directly, then, and he put it to me straight. 'I don't wanna know *why* she wants to meet, jes that she wants to meet.'"

Officer Guerra then went on to explain that one thing I could do, which is a step in this process anyway, is to complete the standard mediation form first. Part of the form includes questions that probe each party's motivations. "Maybe if you fill it out first and sign it, and I show it to him, your assailant will take this as assurance you want to proceed," he speculated.

"Why do you suppose he's doing this?" I asked.

"I can't know what goes on in a prisoner's mind, Mirabelle, but I can tell you Johnson seemed sincere. There was no hint of a punk attitude. Maybe he really doesn't want to relive that event he has spent years trying to forget. I am sure he has only thought about it from his side, though. Thinking about what you have endured has not been part of his mental state, if I were to extrapolate from what I heard and saw."

I needed a few more days to think about this request.

But while he was in front of me, I steered the conversation to an idea I had broached with him only tentatively: Why is a female victim registered with the Victim Notification System in this state not warned in real time if her assailant gets anywhere near her? As parents, we can keep tabs on our kids with GPS smart apps 24/7.

"Good question, Mirabelle. I'm not sure why we can't provide that service. I just know that we do not alert victims in real time in our present system. Not that it's a bad idea. I can see some merit in the possibility."

■ ■ ■ ■ ■

I needed more time to think about this request, so I waited a few days to absorb the implications of taking the next step. "Who the hell does he think he is asking me to do something for *him*?" I asked myself. This attitude stomped around my mind until I realized that if I truly wanted to see him to try and sense any anger he might be harboring toward me, I was going to have to bend my ego and try to turn my fear into energy toward keeping the mediation open. So I took the form and answered the questions as the officer had suggested. My responses were short, simple, and direct.

Apparently, this was not enough to move Johnson to proceed. When Officer Guerra took the forms with my signature to the prison and for the third time attempted to persuade him to meet me, Johnson's demeanor had changed. He was backing out before he even glanced at my responses.

"Mirabelle, he hung his head low and wouldn't look me in the eye. Said, 'Officer, thinking 'bout this meeting done made me sick. Can't sleep. Am depressed. Always nauseated. I jes don't wanna see her. The one person in my family who still talk to me tells me not to do it. Don't think I can handle it. Or should have to. Cellmates done told me not to too. I get out in a few months. Don't need to do this. Ain't gonna do this. But tell her she got nothin' to fear from me.'

"I wasn't surprised at his change of attitude, but I challenged Johnson on your behalf. 'Leroy,' I said, 'I've driven out to this here prison facility three times now, and each time you've told me that meeting Ms. Garrett was the right thing to do. Now you're backing out. Isn't the *real* reason why because you can't face the person you harmed?'

"All he could do, Mirabelle, was to nod his head real slow in agreement with everything I'd said. And the mediation was over."

Officer Guerra relayed this message by phone two weeks after the meeting just in case the inmate had a change of heart. He was surprised that Johnson's cellmates discouraged the mediation because in his decades with Victim Services, most inmates had been positive about the mediation dialogue program. "But I have to tell you, Mirabelle, I've been concerned about his mental state all along. He's been unable to clearly articulate much of anything. He really does seem to want to live a quiet life, and certainly he does not seem to want to see you or interact with you in any way, shape, or form."

I tasted fear bile in my throat. Now I would not know the facial lines of Leroy Johnson. I would not know how he holds himself, his posture, nor would I recognize him by his gait or movements. I would not know him walking down a sidewalk. And, the very worst, I would not recognize him with any of my senses should he approach me. I would have to rely on his repeated declarations to Officer Guerra that he will not harm me. Small comfort when I have been advised to recognize that an imprisoned criminal will say whatever he thinks will get him the best reward at the moment. I cannot rely on Johnson's declarations no matter how sincere they appear to the officer.

I think a concealed handgun license is in my future. My very near future.

30

FORGIVE, NOT FORGET

There is never too much forgiveness to go around. The act of forgiving is instilled in most societies since early childhood. Raised in a Methodist family, I had heard the mantra ever since I could remember. I had not ever been big in the forgiveness department. It was a hard lesson for me to learn—much more demanding than "love one another" or "do unto others." Strength, ambition, and fortitude are my strong suits. And those traits did not often sit side by side with forgiveness.

I had not—in all honesty—really forgiven my father

for failing to lend a hand up the big rumbling bus steps so many decades before. Or all the missed celebrations—birthdays, graduations, and community recognitions—that had an empty seat and an empty hole in my heart when Dad, once again, did not show. I had many opportunities to practice forgiving him, but instead, I leaned on my strong suits and gradually became numb to the slights from him, which ran unabated through my everyday life. When I thought I was strong enough to confront my father about his refusal to help me onto the bus, his reply was pretty predictable from a man raised in the Depression. "Just tryin' to teach you a little character, to get you to get up and do things on your own. I can't believe you even remember that!" End of conversation.

Over the years since the hotel room attack, I had pushed back, struggled, and shoved into dark recesses the prospect of forgiving the angry man who became my enemy. For many years, no great strides were either ventured or gained. But one night an unexpected opportunity for forgiveness sat right down beside me, literally.

■ ▪ ■ ▪ ▪

Henry Gonzales was getting ready for an informal meet and greet with a possible new employer, who was actually a friend of his from way back. So they chose a local bar near the capitol complex. Henry slipped into his

Dockers, loosened his belt a notch, and grabbed his dark brown jacket. He was getting older and disliked that his midsection had gotten wider over the years. But he was still fit overall and had plenty of experience and training in his field. He still looked good.

Henry kissed his wife good-bye and gave her a little wink as he strode out the door. Loving her after all these years was his best fortune in life. She had given him a good family and raised his four children, now, praise God, all grown and out on their own. (He made the sign of the cross and mumbled, "In nomine Patris . . .") He had stood by her throughout her bout with breast cancer. Thank the Lord that he had been employed with a hotel back then that offered great health insurance benefits. Thank the Lord that she survived and was fully recovered. (Henry again made the sign of the cross.)

It was early—about five o'clock—even for happy hour, but he wanted to scope out a good seat with a surrounding view. Henry always wanted to know who was coming in a place and kept his back to a wall if at all possible. In his line of work, anything could change on a dime; besides, some habits die hard.

He sat in the end chair of the bar and ordered a beer. Tall, in a frosted glass. He had a moment to himself, so he settled in to a little reflection. His prospects were good. He was on the shy side of middle age and had kept up his marksman skills on a weekly basis. He was still employed, but the company he worked for was downsizing in this rotten economy and his department felt the pain. It was generous that he had been given sixty days' notice.

Catching the glint of the changing light at the glass entrance door, he looked up to see an attractive professional woman entering the bar.

■ ■ ■ ■ ■

I swept into the room with an air of confidence and familiarity. I was an accomplished lobbyist and could not begin to remember all the stories that had unfolded here. It was a legislative hot spot, and during session, I could easily meet an elected official here in the cool hip space. Meet and drink, that is. My companion was not yet to be seen; in fact, the place was pretty empty—I checked my watch again—and it was still on the early side of happy hour. But there was a guy sitting at the bar. A quick up-and-down look told me he might be good company while I was waiting a bit.

"This seat taken?" He was a little caught off guard, but managed a quick grin.

"Well, young lady, I am waiting on a fellow to join me, but until then, the seat is all yours."

"That makes two of us." I returned the smile. "Hi, my name is Mirabelle." He returned my firm—very firm, in fact—handshake and gave me his full attention. "Henry Gonzales." He was formal, but quick on the comeback,

A Cosmopolitan quickly came up, so an amicable chit-chat easily rolled off my tongue. "Henry or Enrique?" I asked.

"No, not me, but it was my father's name."

We politely bantered back and forth, but the conversation slowed down when Henry shared with me that he was in the security business, mostly with large projects as a team leader. He used to be in the hotel security business but had moved on from that line of work some time back.

I looked into his eyes, hard. "Were you here, in Austin, in 1983?"

"Yes ma'am. I've been here some twenty-five years now."

I glanced at the front door and around the bar to make sure my companion had not slipped in. All clear. I decided—rather impulsively—to share my story. Using a hushed tone and leaning toward him, I unwound the story of my brutal attack. Where it was, the year, the employee having a list of the guests who were women on their own in a single room, and him "wanting to kill a white woman." Henry's eyes grew wider at each turn of the story. His attention was rapt. I noticed that his body language was very still, too still. Something was off.

"It was me," he stammered. "I was in charge of security that night at the hotel."

I gasped. "What?!"

"I was supposed to be there that night. I had gone through all the checkpoints, made sure all of the security equipment was on line and working—which it was. I rarely asked for a night off, but my wife was in the hospital. She had cancer then and I wanted to be with her. I spoke with my deputy guard and he was fine taking over, and the night manager said no problem with me going. I left about eight o'clock.

"I got the call from my deputy about midnight. He had just left your room. He was nearly hysterical. After he calmed down, he told me what he had seen and that he had called the police and an emergency vehicle. The weird thing was that the bartender was already there and there was this other hotel guest there in boxer shorts and laced-up wingtips!"

He paused to collect himself. He was visibly upset.

"He told me it was one of our guys that did this to our guest. It was the new Johnson guy with Maintenance. 'How do you know for sure it's our guy?' I asked him, already wary of a lawsuit. 'She is still alive, she is really beat up, but she is still conscious and is talking. The guest identified her assailant as our guy—he still has on his uniform and name badge.'

"By the time I got back to the hotel, Mirabelle, you were gone. The emergency team had you to the hospital fast. I was there getting the story of the situation down and talking with our bartender and the police when a call came over the radio to let the police look in the room again. We had already locked the door as a crime scene.

"I don't know how, but someone tipped off the police to go back to the room and search for the weapon, a knife. I let the officers in and this time they were on their hands and knees looking for a knife. They had to be careful not to get in all the blood and glass. One of them popped a flashlight under the bed skirt. 'Found it!' he shouted and showed the knife to me. It was not a hotel knife and I told the police that it must be a personal weapon."

Henry leaned toward me. "Mirabelle, I never knew what happened to you after that night. The hospital would not release any information about you. Until this moment, I did not know if you lived or died from that attack—the attack that happened on my watch!" Henry's shoulders began to sag. His eyes were moist. "Mirabelle, this is the nightmare that any of us in the hotel security business dread. This is the fear each of us lives with. This is the event we are supposed to protect our guests from, and I failed at the task. Over all these years, I have asked myself over and over, had I been there and not taken off to see my wife, would this have happened?

"You know, after a few years, I had to quit the security business for hotels. I could not bear the idea that something like that would ever happen to an innocent guest.

"Would you forgive me?"

I softly enclosed my hands over his. He saw the scars that remained on my hand from my defensive wounds. His eyes misted over. I quietly replied, "Henry, it is all right. It's okay. See these? See how they have healed? I have healed, too. I am physically okay. There is no need for you to carry this burden with you any longer. It was not your fault—and I do forgive you. I forgive you with all that I am and still hope to be."

Our eyes met in one more deep exchange. Henry managed a small fleeting smile before the glass door opened and my companion strode inside the bar.

■　■　■　■　■

Forgiveness feels like it's omniscient. I can feel it, but it does not have form. It can be pushed aside from everyday life, hidden in small recesses of the mind. Rarely brought up in casual conversation. Friends don't know about your "forgiveness scorecard," and perhaps they are pretty sure the numbers on their own scorecard are not very high.

As time moved on and the pain of my attack was pushed back into the recesses of my memory, I began to reflect on forgiveness as a method of healing myself. I still could not bring myself to forgive my enemy outright, but I was given some counsel from my closest friend, Lynda. I know I have a wonderful, strong relationship with Lynda, and I find comfort in knowing that she cares very deeply about me. What I did not know, however, is that she has given my emotional healing much thought over the years. She knew that what she wanted to say would be disturbing and might provoke some fissure in our friendship. So she was careful to choose the right time and place to deliver her delicate message.

"What if this isn't entirely about you?"

I was taken aback and hurt by this statement from my trusted friend. Anger flickered in my eyes. "She's betrayed me!" my mind protested as tears began to brim in my eyes.

Lynda lightly tossed her head and gazed directly at me, her Mirabella. "What if your assailant was on a path from God to do this to you? What if he was directed on some level to put himself in your path, hurt you so badly you could see and recognize the Light from the other side but not injure you in a way that would profoundly impact your physical life?

"Think about it. Yes, it was horrible. Yes, it was a crime and he is paying for that crime. But, honestly, how could someone be stabbed repeatedly and not have the knife hit a single internal organ? All the stab wounds were slivered in between your intestines, your kidneys, all of the body parts crucial to your physical well-being. Now how does that happen twelve times?"

I did not have an answer for that. I had been through countless medical exams, each time the physician making a remark very close to this same observation. It was seemingly impossible, but there I stood as living proof in the exam room. And now here. I needed a moment to think, to process what my friend was telling me.

"Can you excuse me for a moment? I want to go to your powder room."

Lynda knew that she did not have to reply. She had anticipated some kind of reaction and trusted me to do the right thing for myself. She got up from the pillows and went to the kitchen to brew some green tea.

I softly closed the bathroom door and braced myself on the basin counter. I closed my eyes for a moment. Opening them, I saw myself in the mirror. "I have been given a Gift, a profound one, a Gift which has emboldened me with a freedom from fear. A Gift which has changed my faith in God to an absolute knowledge that He is here. Right now, throughout time." I turned on the water as much for the sound as for the splash on my face.

I recalled how I felt the suspension of time in Patmos while in His Light. "He reminded me again that He is still very much a part of the plan," I barely whispered. "He cannot make my choices for me, but He has provided me a Gift. What I do with it is my business. My soul journey. Now what?" I looked at my reflection once more. It had never occurred to me to think about my assault in this way. I splashed my face and left to find Lynda, who was still in the kitchen.

Lynda gave me a warm, embracing smile and she gave me a good strong hug.

Then she placed her Kyoto tea service and biscotti on a tray and led us both outside near the soothing water fountain. "Hear me out, please.

"Do you remember the vision I gave to you years ago? The vision given to me, but it was for you? You asked me to inquire about your lifetimes and certain déjà vu remembrances you have experienced. You felt particularly close to angel energies and wanted to have some background on that feeling.

"The sense-feeling I received when you asked that question was that your soul energy is angelic in its essence. You were a strong angel, a vigilant angel in the Father's choir. The Father had commanded that you were to act within certain boundaries. These were clear markers. You understood where you were allowed to play—because on the other side it is play—but during an impulsive moment, you crossed beyond where you were to be. The reason you crossed beyond, however, was to help another entity; there was trouble or pain and you sought to right the wrong. Your motives were grounded in Love. And the vision said to me that your angel energy did shed protective light and prevented pain. But the Father was not pleased. Your soul entity was returned to this planet for a reason. You also remember that we were told that this was to be your last life experience if that is what you want. You have paid your dues. You are forgiven.

"So, as the Father has forgiven you, your work is to learn and experience forgiveness as a human. I know that you have had lots of resentment harbored toward your human father, most of it well deserved. But maybe, just maybe, that was and is your Forgiveness Class 101. Maybe forgiving your negligent and aloof father for being a jerk was and is the precursor to learning a really huge lesson in forgiveness.

"And what if the Father sent your assailant on his life's mission to hurt you only enough so you would have a very-near-death experience, yet come out of it *alive* and *very well*, thank you. In fact, you came out of it financially independent due to the civil settlement from the hotel owners. You know it and I know it. You have achieved a certain lifestyle most people can only imagine. Though you don't flaunt it, you travel, you own your own business, and you pretty much do what you want to do. Is that not a profound gift when you sit back and think about all of it?"

I shifted in her bamboo chair. "You know, it has taken me *years* to get to the physical and emotional point of even considering such an idea. I actually tried to reach out through mediation to try to understand him, his motives, and how I felt. It is meant to be a process of healing for both parties. But he stopped the process; it may have been too much for him to experience. I have been able to come away from that incident more than a survivor; I am a person who has helped other women by changing the law in Texas. I have been a participant in life. But I still keep that thick steel door locked tight between me and the fear and pain inflicted on me that night.

"Now I realize, as years have passed and I have had time to reflect on all of this, that I can feel a small slit in those steel doors. But I also feel I must protect myself because he has been released. Yes, he has a GPS monitoring bracelet on as a condition of parole, but I feel more frightened with him out of jail. I have never wanted to own a firearm, but I do now. I do not know if I could stand down on this, Lynda."

"I understand," she replied in a patient easy voice. "But what if you could break it down into two levels?"

"Okay, let's hear it," I said, knowing that Lynda always had a unique take on situations such as these. I leaned in closer.

"What if he was a messenger? What if he was doing the Father's bidding to get your attention? It would not be the first time the Father inflicted pain on a human to make a point. We know He could do it again.

"Could you forgive the soul of your assailant?"

There. Lynda had laid it on the bottom line. Clearly and succinctly. She always did that for me. I squirmed and pursed my lips.

We each leaned back silently; only the katydids broke the silence. Lynda closed her eyes and gave me some personal energy space to consider her proposition.

"What might that feel like?" I asked Lynda, still

struggling with the ethereal versus the physical concept of forgiveness.

She tilted her head slightly as if she were listening to the other side for guidance. She shook her head.

"I am not hearing anything for that question. But let me tell you what I think as your friend. This whole event and all the events that have surrounded it are beyond normal. There was—and perhaps continues to be—a greater hand in this. For you to truly embrace the Gift provided to you, you must be free of hatred and scorn toward this person. Now, I do not know if I would be strong enough to actually face the man and talk to him. But what I do sense-feel is that he was a bit player in a drama beyond his control. If you are able to accept that, then perhaps you can clear your emotions and your soul energy on a spiritual plane—*that* is your true destination."

I looked at her and let this information sink in. Deep inside, I felt like Lynda was on to something. I still did not know what it would feel like to separate the two energies—human and ethereal—but I thought I might be able to reach within myself to find forgiveness on some level. I also knew that this journey was one my soul was given that will take my lifetime.

■ ■ ■ ■ ■

Okay.

Deep breath.

Exhale.

Enough of this soul-searching spiritual stuff. I need to move on. I can get my heart around forgiving my assailant's soul if he indeed was acting as God's messenger. But I'm a hardheaded, practical Texas woman too.

Right now I gotta blow off some steam, and I know just what to do. I'm going to head out to Daddy's ranch to shoot off some rounds with my newly acquired pink two-toned Smith & Wesson M&P9. I throw my field bag on the floor of my red pickup truck and pop the engine into life. I wave to my neighbors as I lay a little rubber on the asphalt, grinning at my own mischief.

Adíos, and vaya con Dios, y'all!

EPILOGUE

Throughout 2012 Karin Richmond persuaded a small group of politicians and professionals to join her and they began to meet with the staff of the Texas Department of Criminal Justice's Victim Notification System (part of their Victim Services Division) to press them to provide real-time victim notification should a Texas parolee forcibly remove his GPS bracelet or break out of his designated inclusive zone. The following hypothetical story illustrates what might happen as a result of those meetings.

Brenda Naylor lives in San Antonio, Texas, with her family. The year is 2020. She manages a professional team of security personnel for a private company that has contracts in thirty-four states and hundreds of counties to monitor the movements of sexual offenders and violent predatory offenders who are compelled to wear GPS monitoring devices as a condition of parole. Major Naylor gained her surveillance skills while serving with a UN unit during a peacekeeping tour of duty in Egypt in the chaotic period following the Arab Spring. She has contracts with the state of Texas as well as individually with the state's six largest, most populated counties. Her unit is contracted to watch about two thousand parolees.

State and local authorities assign each Super Intensive Supervision Parolee (SISP) an "inclusive zone"—that is, the areas he is permitted to move about in. He also has "exclusive zones" that are prohibited to him, such as schools and parks. If his GPS bracelet registers any breaches, Brenda and members of her staff will be alerted within minutes—in real time.

■ ■ ■ ■ ■

He idly poked at a scab that would not go away. Every time he thought it had healed enough to pull off, he stuck a coat hanger wire down between his ankle bracelet and skin, like he used to do as a kid when he wore a cast.

"I hate this thing," he complained to his roommate in the halfway house. "I hate it especially in the summer and no air-conditioning. It fuckin' itches all the fuckin' time."

"Yeah cholo, but at least you are out of prison, man. That was no goddamn party either."

"Ahh, punta. I wonder if she still lives in that house we used to live in. Didn't have to call the cops, but she did, didn't she? Punta."

His bracelet vibrated and emitted a low buzz. He stared down with blank eyes at the intrusion.

"That's your med call, man."

"What a piece of shit," he mutters to his roommate as he feels the bracelet constricting around his ankle and closes his eyes in anticipation of the drug dose pre-programmed to be administered through a high-powered liquid injection device developed by MIT in 2012 and built right into his bracelet. He also knows that a powerful toxin is embedded and programmed to be released on his skin if he ever tries to break the bracelet off his leg.

But prison will give a man a hell of an education, and he had learned of a retired security guard on the take who might take the bracelet off and give him at *least a day before the GPS signal monitors reported him as missing. All for a hefty price. And he had been saving his money now for nine years. He was ready to teach his punta another lesson, and he planned to hurt her just like they hurt him in prison.*

"She's got it comin' and I plan on giving it to her fast and hard."

■　■　■　■　■

Both hands full, Dahlia pushes the kitchen door open with her back and patiently listens to her two teenagers moan loudly about being late for class. "Turn off the lights and get your lunches, *cariños!*" she calls out. The family piles into their late model Camry and heads down her street in Temple, Texas. Dahlia is pleased with her kids and still praises Mary the mother of Jesus for the subsidized voucher program that got them into a great private school. "We have our lives back now," she says to herself as she glances into the rearview mirror. Her kids, more cheerful now that they are on the road, are smiling right back at her.

But as she merges onto the crosstown freeway, Dahlia starts to get a really bad feeling in her gut. "It was a kind of premonition. I just couldn't shake it off," she would recall later.

When they arrive at the school, she gives her kids an

extra big smile—she had to give up helping them out of the car and hugging them in front of their friends some time ago—and she turns back into the traffic to get to her workplace. It is a local bank branch and she likes her hard-won position as a clerk. She also feels safe because she knows that there are security cameras throughout the building. Although it has been years since her ex-boyfriend raped and assaulted her, she still is not completely free of her memories and fear. "I'm not sure I or anyone else can truly get over horror and violence," she has confided to a close friend at work.

Years ago, when he first entered the prison system, Dahlia had taken precautions to protect herself and her kids from her former boyfriend and their father. The Texas Department of Criminal Justice had encouraged her to participate in their Victim Notification System— part of the Victim Services Division—and she had provided her cell phone and email address. She also had her phone receive her email so she would not miss much if she was off line for a while.

In the odd moment, she remembered how astonished she was when she first officially signed up to be contacted if her assailant—she called him "a predator"—ever intentionally broke out of his inclusive zone or forcibly cut off his bracelet, to learn that she would not be called immediately. Her only notification from the Texas Department of Criminal Justice would be through the U.S. Postal Service. "Incredible! Even a decade ago, I knew where my kids were pretty much 24/7 with the GPS app on their cell phones!" she said to herself.

Then last year, to her surprise, she opened a letter and even got a robo-call on her cell phone with good, really good, news. Texas was starting a new program to contact victims registered with the Notification System if their assailant paroled with a GPS monitoring device broke free of his electronic boundaries. And the victim would be notified within *fifteen minutes* of the time the parole system discovered the violation.

Dahlia did not hesitate to sign up. When she called Victim Services, she found out that she could elect to have a "call out option" for her cell phone or an "SMS texting" notification on any cell or email address she liked. She was warned, however, that since the system was new to Texas, there may be some false alarms. But the staff eased her concerns when they shared that this service was already in place in a dozen or so states and run by a private security company that had a contract throughout the nation. "So they know what they're doing," assured the state deputy. Dahlia was not dissuaded by their warning, and signed on the real-time notification option that very day.

■ ■ ■ ■ ■

Brenda Naylor's San Antonio security unit is a hive of muffled activity. One of her team leaders is asking about a new protocol when a signature audible tone rings out on the floor. The open room is low light and oversized screens are within reach for all the staff. Fingers fly on several transparent screens. "Major Naylor, it looks like we have a GPS breach in Houston!" She quickly moves to the screen and pulls up the parolee background. "Ortiz, Felipe. Rapist; child endangerment and assault. Out of Houston. Parole Officer Lincoln."

Her words are clipped as she gives the order. "Notify Officer Lincoln, now. We need boots-on-the-ground intel immediately."

Moments later, Officer Lincoln is on the secure line hearing the bad news. "Parolee Ortiz appears to have broken out of his safe zone. Can you confirm?"

"He is not due to check in for an hour," Officer Lincoln replied. "Where do his GPS coordinates put him?"

Brenda pings the coordinates to his handheld secure device. "On it," confirming receipt of the location data.

A red warning button flashes slowly on the incident screen. This indicates that the system is in a countdown process to call and text the registered victim associated with the parolee. Protocol dictates that she wait for a few minutes to receive physical intel from Officer Lincoln. Lincoln pings her back on the system, confirming the parolee's absence and that he had no permission to be outside the inclusive area. Brenda touches the red button to accelerate the call that will go out automatically in eight more minutes.

Dahlia nearly jumps out of her seat when she hears the distinct tone reserved for victim notifications. Petrified, not only for herself but for her children, she manages to calmly share with her boss what is transpiring and leaves the bank within minutes to head to the school. She calls her children on the way and tells them not to ask questions but to meet her at the front of the school in a few minutes. "Do not leave the inside of the building until you see our car and see me and then come out quickly," she says, trying hard to keep her voice from shaking. She battled within herself as to whether she would tell her children the gravity of their situation. They had not had any connection with their father, and she thought this was an especially bad time to start. She decided to take the advice she had received from the professional staff at SafeHome, where she had already registered herself and her children as victims so they would know them should Dahlia ever get this dreaded call-out.

Safely inside the shelter for victims of assault, the counselors were with Dahlia's son and daughter, and she waited alone in a room, oblivious to the colorful art expressions of the youngsters who had found a home in this place. Nothing else to do but wait, and pray to her Lord.

Padre nuestro que estás en los cielos
Santificado sea tu Nombre
Venga tu reino
Hágase tu voluntad
En la tierra como en el cielo
Danos hoy el pan de este día
y perdona nuestras deudas
como nosotros perdonamos nuestros deudores
y no nos dejes caer en al tentación
sino que líbranos del malo.
Amen.

Major Brenda Naylor would be late for dinner, but she stayed on-site waiting for some snippet of information about parolee Ortiz. Her patience was rewarded with a call from Officer Lincoln.

"We found Ortiz. He had made it as far as outside Temple. We put an APB out and the local PD located him near Interstate 35, heading north," he reported in military fashion. Brenda relaxed and absently rubbed the back of her tired neck.

"When he realized the officers were closing in, he pulled out a weapon and shot in their direction. The officers returned fire. He's dead, Major."

"Thank you, Officer Lincoln. We will send out the appropriate notifications."

Brenda touched the red flashing button on the screen and made the personal call to Dahlia. It was the best call she had made in a long time.

ACKNOWLEDGMENTS

This book has been thirty years in the writing, and I am indebted to many friends, family members, and colleagues who have helped me tell my story. I am especially grateful to Senator Juan Hinojosa for lending his ear and taking a chance on a very young and untried advocate for economic development. Very early readers of my manuscript who edited for love and encouraged me include my dear friends Sylvia de Leon and Yvette Reynolds. Belle provided exceptional insight and challenged me to tug out my emotions even though it hurt. Carrington McDuffie also offered gentle guidance. A special thanks goes to Pastor Mike Robertson at Riverbend Church in Austin. His Scribe class placed me among other writers in a secure and emotionally safe environment so I could dig deeper and pick up the writing I had left on the shelf for five years.

And thanks to the people who took the time to circle back to events in their distant past and share their recollections and perspectives of events described in the novel. You know who you are.

The Texas Department of Criminal Justice's Victim Services Division has been a constant force for good over these years. While the staff might state they are just doing their job, I know Ms. McCown's team is compassionate and respectful of women victimized by violent crimes.

And certainly not least, I would like to thank the wonderful staff of Greenleaf Book Group for their support of my story and for providing me with the gracious and tenacious editor Linda O'Doughda.

ABOUT THE AUTHOR

Karin Richmond is one of eight Texans and the only Texas woman recognized for extraordinary achievement as a fellow member of the International Economic Development Council. She sits on two national editorial boards and is a thought leader in the field of tax incentive policy. She resides with her extended family in Austin, Texas. This is her first novel.